Wisconsin's Ghosts

Sherry Strub

Schiffer Publishing Ltd ®

4880 Lower Valley Road, Atglen, Pennsylvania 19310

Other Schiffer Books by Sherry Strub:

Milwaukee Ghosts, ISBN: 978-0-7643-2866-4, $12.95
Ghosts of Madison, Wisconsin, ISBN: 978-0-7643-3072-8, $14.99

Storm Over Sherwood Point © Robert Goode. Image from BigStockPhotos.com

Designed by Stephanie Daugherty
Type set in Rosemary Roman/New Baskerville BT

ISBN: 978-0-7643-3209-8
Printed in United States of America

Published by Schiffer Publishing, Ltd.
4880 Lower Valley Road
Atglen, PA 19310
Phone: (610) 593-1777; Fax: (610) 593-2002
E-mail: Info@schifferbooks.com

For our complete selection of fine books on this and related subjects, please visit our website at www.schifferbooks.com. You may also write for a free catalog.

This book may be purchased from the publisher. Please try your bookstore first.

We are always looking for people to write books on new and related subjects. If you have an idea for a book, please contact us at proposals@schifferbooks.com

Schiffer Publishing's titles are available at special discounts for bulk purchases for sales promotions or premiums. Special editions, including personalized covers, corporate imprints, and excerpts can be created in large quantities for special needs. For more information, contact the publisher.

In Europe, Schiffer books are distributed by
Bushwood Books
6 Marksbury Ave.
Kew Gardens
Surrey TW9 4JF England
Phone: 44 (0) 20 8392 8585; Fax: 44 (0) 20 8392 9876
E-mail: info@bushwoodbooks.co.uk
Website: www.bushwoodbooks.co.uk

Dedication

To George and Audrey Ferkey
and Ted and Shirley Strub.

Acknowledgements

A big thank you to Craig Strub and Nikki Linzmeier. I truly couldn't have done it without your support. Thanks to all the people who spoke to me in person, by phone, and e-mail. A special thanks to Andrew Kirkpatrick, Joe Bachman, Michelle Laucke, Karen and Don Rathke, Vicky and Phil Elsing, Noah Leigh and the rest of the PIM team, Mary Sutherland, Wayne Hackler, Scotty Rorek and the MRIP team, Stacy Kopchinski, Pam Booth, Bob Kaiser, Dan Johns, Ruth Forrest Glenn, Janelle Peterson, Karla Schuessler, Karla Houghton, Marty, Sheri Reading, Angie Seidl, Jim Villiesse, and the New London Public Museum staff. And last but not least, my fantastic editor, Dinah Roseberry.

Author's Note

Please remember to ask permission before entering any private residence, cemetery after hours, etc. If "No Trespassing" signs are posted, respect them!

Contents

Section Two: Central Wisconsin Ghosts 55

Contents

Section Three: Southern Wisconsin Ghosts......................149

9

Section Four: Attractions and Of Ghostly Interest 201

Of Ghostly Interest **209**

Bibliography **213**

Index **217**

Introduction

On Wisconsin...Ghosts!

Wisconsin—home of the Packers, Harley Davidson, too many breweries to count, lakes, cranberries, potatoes, cheese, and of course, Cheeseheads! But this is only scratching the surface of what Wisconsin is and what Wisconsin has to offer.

Beautiful lakes, farms, countryside, tourist attractions—natural and supernatural...Wisconsin is a visual feast of what we see and sometimes can't see—ghosts.

If you think Wisconsinites are a unique bunch when they're alive, believe me when I say they're just as unique dead.

Wisconsin's ghosts come from every nook and cranny of this great state. Some are timid; some are bold. Some are human; some are animal. And some are downright frightening in whatever visible or invisible shape they take.

Among Wisconsin's ghosts: a legless milkmaid, ghosts that toss desks across a classroom, Civil War ghosts, little girl and boy ghosts... Wisconsin's ghosts are Native American, former slaves, Swedish, angry, happy, men, women, cows, chickens, and cats. Apparently most ghosts don't know they're dead because they just keep on doing what they did when they were living, breathing humans, regardless of how much shock their appearance might cause.

The ghosts of Wisconsin in this book are divided into three geographical areas: northern, central, and southern. The ghosts of the north are first, followed by the ghosts of central Wisconsin, and finally the ghosts of southern Wisconsin. If your city is close to one of the imaginary lines, check the section above or below. If you don't see your city listed—sorry. Maybe next time.

So read on. But keep in mind that Wisconsin's Ghosts will stay with you long after you put down this book.

1

Northern Wisconsin Ghosts

City 1: Antigo

McMillion Hotel

This hotel, built in 1887, no longer exists. However, before the building was razed in August, 2007, a whole lotta deaths, the rumored number is 18, supposedly took place here.

The ghostly presence could have been anyone, but one likely candidate is a former owner who killed himself in Room 21 of the hotel. Mr. E.N. Mellor was said to have become so distraught after reading his mail that he killed himself. The day he stopped living was December 22, 1892.

Another ghost said to haunt the hotel before it was razed: Mr. Muller, a partner in the lumber company, Hoxie & Muller. He also committed suicide at the hotel. The reason could be that the lumber company burned eighteen months earlier. It should be noted that Hoxie, his partner, didn't stick around after Muller died. He moved to California.

The ghostly activity in the hotel included footsteps, doors opening and closing, and apparitions. Dark shadows were seen by many. These same dark shadows may be responsible for the "pushing" some felt when they were in certain places in the building.

This hotel, formerly located at 520 Superior Street in downtown Antigo, was also known as the Vivian Hotel, the Farrell Hotel, the Schneiter Hotel, and the McMillion Hotel.

City 2: Amery

Old Lutheran Church

This old church is…old. Built almost 140 years ago, it stands about five miles outside of Amery. Norwegian settlers were the first to worship here.

The bell was said to begin ringing on its own back in 1981. The pastor of the church could hear it when she was across the street in the parsonage. No one was in the church when the bell would ring. Of course, the church was investigated. Of course, no bell ringer could be found. At least no human bell ringer. Since that time, the church bell has been frequently heard ringing when the church is empty.

Bell ringing isn't the only thing the church has going on. There's the sound of whispers coming from the wooden pews, and the sound of whispers and muted words coming from inside the walls themselves.

Some theorize a few of the former members of the church are still stopping by to worship. A cemetery is nearby, but so far, no one has seen or heard anything unearthly there.

City 3: Argonne

Old Argonne Grade School

This school closed in the 1990s, was later condemned, and finally destroyed by fire. After the school was closed, area children would go upstairs and write their names on the wall. In this same upstairs area was a storage room where a janitor was said to have hung himself.

During these upstairs forays, children would see a man hanging from the rafter. Instead of seeing him as a ghost; they saw him as clearly as if he were alive. Not a pretty sight, I'm guessing.

But not everyone saw the dead janitor; some only heard him moaning as if he were in pain.

The school is no longer there, but there are those that swear they see lights on where the building used to stand. The school was located on Highway 55. Now there's nothing more than a dirt driveway leading to where the building once existed. If you so desire, you can try to see the lights. Take Highway 32 north to Argonne. Once in town, take a right on Highway 55, which is also Bailey Avenue. The old school would have been on the right. Look for a dirt/gravel road...and a light.

City 4: Ashland

Hotel Chequamegon

This breathtaking hotel, located on the south shores of Lake Superior at 101 Lake Shore Drive West, is rumored to be haunted. If ghosts do haunt the hotel, they have plenty of room. There are sixty-five Victorian-style rooms.

The hotel is relatively new, so it's anyone's guess who is responsible for the sound of voices when no one's around and cold drafts in rooms that are otherwise warm.

Northland College

Memorial Hall on the Northland College campus, located at 1411 Ellis Avenue, is said to be haunted by current and former students.

The reason? A former student is said to have committed suicide in the 1920s or 1930s by jumping—not falling—down a three-story elevator shaft. The girl ghost, who has been seen as both a ghost and ghostly mist, and felt as a cold draft of air, is said to dislike men.

There are many on campus that theorize that this unfortunate girl did not jump into the elevator shaft; she may have been pushed by a boyfriend. Sooty black handprints have been found on walls after rooms have been opened in the morning. This is after the rooms have been cleaned the night before.

Computers also turn on by themselves in certain rooms in the school and then print whatever is on the desktop. Apparently the ghosts are techies.

But this isn't the only story associated with Northland College. In the 1920s, a student who was afraid he wasn't meeting his father's expectations was said to have committed suicide in the basement of Woods Hall. A groaning sound, like a rope under a heavy load, straining against a beam was heard in the basement of Woods Hall. Soft, shuffling footsteps were also heard in the building when no one was there. Woods Hall was torn down in 1970, but that may not be the end of the story, or the ghost. Some say he moved to another building on campus.

Rinehart Theater

The costume room located in the upstairs of the theater is where footsteps can be heard. You guessed it—no human is attached to them. A female theater director was said to have seen the headless body of a ghost with its back to her. One can only imagine what she might have seen if the ghost had turned around.

During performances, cast members have seen the door to the dressing room open, heard the downstairs toilet flush, and have also seen the door close by itself.

The theater is located at 210 5th Avenue East.

Soo Line Depot

The Soo Line Depot, also known as Union Depot, is located at Third Avenue West at Fourth Street. Though it's no longer used as a transportation depot, some spirits haven't transported their carcasses off the premises.

15

The huge brownstone building is listed in both the State and National Register of Historic Places. As the building was undergoing renovations a couple of years ago, an unearthly visitor dropped by for a visit.

When workers were working on the concrete, one went down to the basement. He saw someone standing there and asked, "How did you get down here so fast?" The worker turned around for a second. When he looked back, the someone that had been standing there was gone. Freaked out, he raced upstairs and told the others that they weren't going to believe him, but he saw a man in 1890s clothing that included a starched collar. The worker went on to describe the rest of the ghost: He had a body but no face. Apparently the ghost wanted to visit the depot incognito.

The worker's story made an impression. No one else would go downstairs alone after that. No word of any other faceless ghost sightings.

City 5: Baldwin

County Road YY

The first part of this story comes from Michelle, a former resident of Baldwin. "When I moved to St. Croix County, there was the continued presence of a Native American in the vicinity of County Road YY. I caught daytime glimpses of a man with his shirt off and jet black hair, and he made me think of cowboy and Indian stories from the old wild west, by his attire. It was always a walking-away glimpse and so slight I wondered if I had imagined it."

If this witness imagined the ghost, she's not alone. Others have also seen Native Americans dressed in 1800s attire in this same area that disappear as you approach. Lifelike yet ghostly lumberjacks have also been seen walking alongside this county road.

City 6: Bayfield

Michigan Island Lighthouse

Surprise! The Michigan Island Lighthouse is located on Michigan Island. The first light station was built in 1857 and the details surrounding its origins are as mysterious as the ghost said to haunt the lighthouse. The lighthouse was never mentioned until 1857 in a report. It's assumed it was built by a Milwaukee firm because they were commissioned to build a lighthouse. However, in the report, no mention of a location was listed, so the Milwaukee builders may have built a lighthouse on Michigan Island by mistake when the intended spot was La Pointe on Madeline Island. Or it may be that someone may have been trying to get two lighthouses built for the price of one. We'll probably never know the answer.

The station was reported to have been completed in late 1856. It was a small whitewashed stone building, with a story-and-a-half keeper's dwelling attached. The stone tower was sixty-four feet high and capped with an octagon-shaped cast iron lantern.

This is where the story gets very interesting. The contractors submitted the lighthouse to the district inspector for his approval—except the inspector didn't approve the lighthouse because it didn't conform to the terms of the contract.

The lighthouse was empty for about ten years until authorities, out of the blue, expressed a desire to reactivate it.

Life at the lighthouse was said to be uneventful for about thirty years, until keeper John Pasque escaped—yes, escaped—injury when the lighthouse lantern was struck by lightning in 1889. The lightning bolt followed the cast iron spiral staircase to the cement floor where it shattered.

A list of subsequent keepers reveals no deaths inside the lighthouse. The new Michigan Lighthouse was built in 1929 when the original, and some say haunted, lighthouse became obsolete.

Stories say the ghost that haunts the lighthouse and surrounding grounds is a former lighthouse keeper who was killed during a bad storm. It's said that a heavy metal door slammed shut on him, ending his life. The only problem is that no former lighthouse keeper that I could find was killed during a storm. But that, of course, does not mean a lighthouse keeper or assistant that died elsewhere has not returned to the lighthouse after death.

It's said that one of the lighthouse doors slams twice during bad storms. This would be incredibly scary on its own, but even more so when you realize that the door slams twice even if it's bolted shut.

Theodore Ernst House

The beautiful old house, built in 1885 by Theodore Ernst, stands at 17 North Fourth Street in Bayfield. You cannot help but be struck by the home's splendor. It sports ornate lace trim carpentry like nobody's business.

In a tower that is not accessible from the house, a figure is often seen at the window. Some see the figure as a woman, some say it is a mist, others say it is a drifting form.

The house is a stop on the very popular Haunted Bayfield Ghost Walk. See the Attractions section for more information.

City 7: Boulder Junction

Headwaters Restaurant & Tavern

Once known as Old Tavern, this gathering place is located on the Manitowish River at 5675 County M.

A ghost called Red Lady is said to haunt the tavern. The building is one of the oldest in town and was opened in the 1930s. The current owner bought the establishment about ten years ago and has been busy making improvements ever since.

Red Lady is said to be the wife of a former owner. She makes an occasional in-person appearance, but usually makes herself known as a cold breeze. She also likes to hide your things.

Stevenson Creek Ruins

County M in Boulder Junction seems to have it going on—at least when it comes to ghosts. This haunted former log mansion was built about 1905, approximately four miles south of the city of Boulder Junction. Stevenson Creek flows beneath Hwy M and is close to Trout Lake. The ruins of the home, which was once considered the most magnificent in the north woods, lie on the north shore of the creek.

In 1905, the site didn't have many trees, unlike most other places in northern Wisconsin. Loggers had done what they do best: They left the area bereft of most trees. On the other hand, this left a magnificent view of the creek from the house. Arthur L. Stevenson and his family lived in the big house from 1905 to 1911. Stevenson had four children: Ruth, Rolland, Raymond, and Esther. Arthur died in 1938.

The family had originally planned to use Stevenson Creek as part of their cranberry business. Unfortunately, the land wasn't particularly suited for cranberry growing because it had too many slopes. Stevenson was said to have abandoned his efforts at growing cranberries at Stevenson Creek in about 1915.

The state bought all the property and tore down the mansion for its logs. (Incredibly, a few miles up the road is one of the largest cranberry-growing areas in the world.)

Ghosts have been seen entering the foundation of the mansion that no longer exists and also entering the building—but the building sometimes looks as it did back in 1905. When you hurry toward the building to see what is going on, the mansion changes back to its current state—abandoned and decaying.

Many people have reported feeling a cool wind near the ruins, even when all else is calm. A multitude of ghosts, children, and adults, have been reported in this area. The ghost of Mr. Stevenson has been spotted walking along the edge of the creek while his children play nearby.

City 8: Cameron

Betty's Café

This very haunted café is located at 706 Main Street in Cameron. The two-story building was moved from its old location to its present location about a hundred years ago.

Bob Kaiser has owned the café since 1986, and has been living upstairs for about two or three years. He said he has never personally seen or heard any ghosts in the building, but said some people came from Eau Claire to check into any possible paranormal activity. Did they find any? Yes.

Kaiser also says, "My cook swears up and down that she feels a ghostly presence." The ghostly presence is said to be a former worker who spent a lot of time by the fryer. She died of a heart attack, but likes the place so much that she keeps hanging around.

Objects are also said to go missing and then reappear in odd places. Some customers believe there's another ghost here. They say it's a regular.

Betty's Café serves up some excellent food. Stop by if you're in the area to check out their menu. If you're lucky, you might spot at least one ghost.

City 9: Canton

Pioneer Rest Cemetery

By day, shadows might follow you. By night, you might see apparitions. If you're lucky (maybe not the right word), you might see the little girl ghost said to sit in a tree inside the graveyard.

This final resting place, also known as Bantley Graveyard, has a number of stories attached to it that involve satanic rituals and cult activity. Many are said to visit the graveyard at night, so if you're looking to meet up with an apparition, you might just get more than you bargained for.

The reason Pioneer Rest Cemetery is better known as Bantley Graveyard is because of one particular story attached to the cemetery. A man named Bantley was said to have murdered his wife and their four children in the cemetery, and when he was finished, he walked to the barn next to the cemetery and hung himself.

Another scary story associated with this cemetery is about two boys who were found dead there. They were running around like boys do, when a hand reached up out of a grave and grabbed one boy by the leg. He died of fright. His brother was also found dead outside the cemetery; no cause of death mentioned.

Unfortunately, vandals recently entered the cemetery, smashed urns, kicked over stones, and destroyed gravestones beyond repair.

If the ghosts were restless before, they are more than likely way past that now. So are the humans that live nearby. A note to ghost hunters: Please treat the dead with respect. Like it or not, you'll be dead one day, too.

City 10: Chippewa Falls

Amy's Ritz

The spot where Amy's Ritz now stands is said to have been a launderette. This launderette, owned by a Chinese man, burned down with him in it. The ghost of the Chinese man has been seen standing in one corner of the bar by patrons.

Amy's Ritz, Chippewa Fall.

This story may be just that—a story—because the building is known to have existed for more than 120 years.

Another story, much different than the first, involves a short ghost that the owner, Amy Anderson, and her father have both spotted in the bar—though not simultaneously.

The first time Anderson saw the ghost, she was very hot from mopping the floor. Suddenly, she felt a cold gust of air. When she turned around, she saw a short man facing the basement. She blinked, looked again, and the man had disappeared.

Anderson's father later saw a short man, too, but the man he saw was brown; the shade wasn't mentioned.

One Amy's Ritz employee wouldn't go into the basement alone. Apparently this fear didn't transfer to anyone else. The place was crowded when I visited town.

The door to the upstairs apartment is also said to lock on its own, and items go missing and turn up somewhere else. Amy's Ritz is located at 114 West River Street.

Eagles Club

Located at 2588 Hallie Road, this building is widely believed to be haunted by a woman who had a heart attack and died there in 1985. The ghost is called Beth. She was said to be only sixty-five years old when she died. Is it any wonder she's still kicking up her heels at the Eagles Club?

James Sheeley House Saloon and Restaurant

Now a saloon/restaurant, the Sheeley House, which has been serving the Chippewa Valley in one capacity or another for more than 100 years, was once one of 30 boarding houses that served lumberjacks, adventurers, and railroaders.

James Sheeley, an Irish immigrant, and his wife, Kate, bought the property in 1905. James tended bar, while Kate and their children kept up the rooms and prepared meals. James died in 1913; Kate rented rooms and prepared meals, but leased the saloon. When Kate died in 1934, the Sheeleys' daughter, Anna, continued renting rooms, but stopped serving meals. In 1981, Anna finally left her home of more than seventy years.

Later, David and Sharon Raihle began reconstruction and restoration of the building; Jim Bloms purchased the beautiful red-brick building in 2001.

Footsteps have been heard by employees on the stairs when they close up at night, but this building is probably best known for the roses

James Sheeley House Saloon and Restaurant, Chippewa Falls.

painted on the wall that were part of its earlier décor. When the roses were painted over, they would "bleed" through. Further attempts to paint over the roses would yield the same results.

The ghost might have an agenda. Once, an employee who went to the attic was locked inside when the door closed behind him. To top it off, the lights shut off...with no help from the hapless employee. Luckily, he was able to get out a half hour later—with the help of a pick. The handsome building is located at 236 West River Street.

City 11: Clear Lake

Moe Church

Moe Lutheran Church is located at 451 30th Street in Clear Lake. Both the church and cemetery are said to be haunted. Legend has it that the church was accidentally burned to the ground in the early 1900s, trapping more than thirty people inside.

When the church was rebuilt, it was said to come with some extras— ghosts. A young woman has been seen in the bell tower and in the cemetery, clutching a baby to her chest. This woman is said to have hung herself after her baby died.

The road between the church and cemetery is also said to be haunted. Ghosts have been blamed for many accidents on this stretch of road. No one is sure if the ghosts of those that burned in the fire are responsible for the hauntings, or if it's the suicidal woman.

City 12: Cornell

Cornell Public Library

The ghosts said to reside in the basement of this Chippewa County library most likely aren't there to read or check out the newest books on the shelf.

The library was once a jail in Cornell's early days. The spiritual presence is said to be attached to former inmates. The former bathroom area in the basement was said to ooze bad vibes; so much so that some librarians were said to be reticent to go downstairs.

I was recently told by library staff that the bathroom is now located upstairs. I was also told nicely by the same employee that she had worked at the library for ten years and had never seen a ghost.

The library is located at 117 North 3rd Street.

City 13: Couderay

Al Capone's Hideout

Like many other Wisconsin homes and businesses associated with Capone, this cabin overlooking Cranberry Lake is believed to be haunted by the ghost of Capone himself. To top it off, Cranberry Lake is haunted even without Capone because of those who have drowned in the lake over the years.

The cabin, built on 400 acres, is reminiscent of a fortress. It may outwardly look like a vacation getaway, but it is said to be more suited to a literal getaway.

The main lodge of the estate has eighteen-inch thick walls. Machine gun portals were built into the wall with a machine gun turret overlooking the entrance. Trespassers beware!

Al Capone's ghost has been spotted inside the lodge. Others—could be members of Capone's gang or even a rival gang—have been spotted in the woods around the hideout. Some wonder if these ghosts are enemies that were disposed of in the lake that have decided to dry off on land.

Cool tidbit of info: There's even a one-man prison on the site. No reports of a ghost in the prison. So far.

City 14: Crivitz

The Pines Supper Club

Located on the shores of beautiful Crooked Lake, this supper club doesn't look haunted. And it isn't. Maybe. But the lake right behind it is.

A ghostly old fishing boat has been spotted at night and during the day. Usually, the boat is located near the middle of the lake, but sometimes it's closer to the supper club.

A ghostly man is said to call for help. Just as you're ready to take action, the boat and the man disappear into a mist. The Pines Supper Club is located in Oconto County at 15375 County W.

City 15: Evergreen Township

Sherry Cemetery

This cemetery in Langlade County near the town of Elton is the site of strange lights that seem to come out of the woods at you, as well as strange noises.

Like most other cemeteries, the Sherry Cemetery has the usual mix of old and new graves. No identity has been attached to the ghost said to haunt the cemetery. However, this ghost definitely wants to be left alone.

One nocturnal visitor said he went there to "check things out" and left his dog in the car with the window down about six inches. About five minutes later, he got a really creepy feeling. At almost the exact same time, his dog started barking. Before he could yell at the dog, it squeezed through the window, fell to the ground with a yelp and raced toward him, presumably to "save" him.

He said he turned around to see why his dog was acting so crazed and saw a blob of blue-white light. He said he instantly started running toward the car. The dog raced past and collided with the light. The dog let out a painful yelp and hobbled back to the car.

When the visitor turned around the light was gone. He opened the car door, the dog jumped in the back and buried its head under a pile of his belongings.

City 16: Fifield

Forest Home Cemetery

This cemetery, also called Fifield Cemetery, is said to be a hotbed of paranormal activity. Orbs, ectoplasm mists, and shadows have all been reported swirling around particular gravestones.

Voices, particularly at night when no one else is around, are said to call out from behind gravestones between you and the entrance. No specific examples of what the voices are saying, however.

Perhaps the most interesting thing about this cemetery is the ball of fire that was witnessed above the cemetery seventy years ago. The cemetery is located on Old Highway 70.

Holy Cross Road

The road lies between Fifield and Phillips off Old Highway 13. If you're heading north, take a right, which is east.

In addition to apparitions of a woman who was said to have been killed by a train at the Wisconsin Central train track crossing, people have reported seeing gnomes. That's right. Gnomes.

Most people who have come to the area say, even if they don't see anything ghostlike, that they feel "gobs" of icy air swirl around them even in the dead of summer.

The woman's ghost has been seen hovering over a pond near the tracks and she has been seen on the tracks themselves. Some say this is her way of trying to keep others from the same fate.

In addition to the ghostly woman, children ghosts have been seen playing in a nearby field.

City 17: Goodrich

School, Tavern, Church and More

This town, listed as a "ghost town," lies between Medford and Merrill on Highway 64, tucked into the southeast corner of Taylor County, and has a population of less than 500. Paranormal activity in the unincorporated town exists in the form of strange lights coming from the foundation of an old school there.

Also said to be haunted are an old tavern and church that are not much more than foundations themselves. Old-time lumberjack ghosts have been seen walking tiredly down Rustic Road during the twilight hours.

In several places in town, the sound of children's voices can be heard.

City 18: Gresham

The Novitiate

This is one historical event that took in place in Wisconsin that is worth learning more about, even if you don't see the word "ghost" in any of your reading.

The Novitiate was a breathtaking mansion when it was built in 1939 by Jennie Peters for her invalid daughter, Jane. The ghostly presence that is said to haunt what's left of the Novitiate could be any one of a number of people—I'll get to that in a minute—but the ghost is most likely Jennie or Jane, though Jane died before she was able to live there. Jennie Peters lived there until 1948.

The Novitiate was gifted to the Alexian Brothers in 1950. What a gift! It should be noted that Peters had the building built according to certain specifications so that it could one day be donated to the Alexian Brothers; Jennie Peter's late husband had formed a high regard for the Alexian Brothers while he lived in Chicago, hence the reason for handing the building over.

First things first. The Alexian Brothers aren't there now. They put the property up for sale in 1969. Unfortunately, a sale was never made. In 1974, a group of Green Bay Indians entered into negotiations to lease the facility as an alcohol and rehabilitation center.

Just as all the plans were about to be finalized, a dissident group of Indians calling themselves the Menominee Warrior Society seized the property along with a cry of "Deed or Death." This was a big deal back in those days; historians and those that remember the event say it still is.

Two months passed. The situation was becoming dire; the threat of violence escalated with each passing day. The Alexian Brothers finally reached an agreement with the Menominee Warrior Society. They would sell the building to the Menominee Tribe for one dollar. Incredibly, five months after the Menominee takeover, the tribe relinquished ownership of the facility because of lack of funds, support, and plans. The Alexian Brothers went ahead with plans to try to sell the elegant building to someone else.

On October 12, 1975, a fire in the building gutted the mansion, but left the dormitory mostly intact. It was never determined if the fire was accidental or if it was started by an arsonist. On November 13, 1975, the Alexian Brothers gave the Novitiate to a different party. It changed hands numerous times after that.

In 2003, the Novitiate addition was torn down; in 2005, the property was divided and offered for sale. The mansion is an empty shell now, but those who have visited the property say there is a definitely spiritual presence, whether that of one of the Peters, or perhaps one or more of the novitiates that came here to prepare for life after the novitiate.

City 19: Hayward

Book World

What kind of person can go into a book store, go directly to what they came there for, pay for it, and walk out? Not anyone I know—that's the beauty of a book store, you can linger as long as you like, while you look through books, before you make a decision.

I'm thinking that goes for ghosts, too. Book World in Hayward is believed to have its own resident ghost. The smell of someone smoking a pipe can be smelled when no one is, or has been, smoking. It's not hard to picture some ghostly well-read tobacco aficionado checking to see what's new on the shelves alongside a real-live book lover.

One woman was even said to have issued a warning to the invisible pipe smoker: "Don't burn the books!"

Book World is located at 10553 S Main St # J.

Ghost Island

It doesn't get any ghostlier than Ghost Island. A whole island is named for the ghosts said to reside here, and they're not happy ghosts. They are believed to be very angry Sioux warriors who died during battle there. The island also has other names you might have heard: Bone Island and Strawberry Island.

Though fishing and the great outdoors are the primary reason people visit Hayward, many fishermen find they can't stay longer than fifteen minutes when they are near the island.

For years and years, strange sounds and apparitions have been seen and heard coming from the island. Photos have been taken of ghostly shapes that were moving against the wind.

There are many theories about the ghost or ghosts that inhabit this uninhabited island, and most center around the Ojibwa. The island could be a tribal burial ground, and the spirits could be those of tribal members.

While many try to explain away the years of ghostly sights and sounds, the reports keep coming in. Nearby residents hope developers stay away; development on the island may cause an extreme reaction from the already-restless residents of Ghost Island.

Lac Courte Oreilles Casino

The gaming, lodge, and convention center rests on what used to be a farm. The farmhouse was said to be haunted even before it was moved to its current location about a mile down the road. Apparently, the ghosts like the casino better, because they seem to have stuck around.

Workers at night have seen apparitions in the casino after it is closed and everyone is gone. So far, the ghosts have not been seen playing poker, slots, roulette, or blackjack.

The casino, which will be sixteen years old this year, is located at 13767 West County Road B.

City 20: Hudson

Liquor Store and Restaurant

This building is located on Coulee Road, very near where the haunted Paschal Aldrich home once stood. So close, in fact, that the owner of this establishment believes she has seen Paschal on a couple of occasions on site.

The owner also witnessed a ghostly event that occurred inside her restaurant. She was standing in the kitchen with some of her staff and had a clear view of the restaurant. While they were looking toward the restaurant, a wine glass fell from the wine rack. Not an unusual occurrence in a restaurant—unless it floats across the carpet for a significant distance and then falls on the floor and breaks.

Paschal Aldrich Home

Paschal Aldrich's ghost is said to haunt his former home on Coulee Road, just off the Interstate in Hudson, a scenic town near the Minnesota border. But he may not be the only ghost in residence…

The story doesn't really begin with Paschal; it begins with his father, Dr. Philip Aldrich. The elder Aldrich was a wealthy entrepreneur. Less driven Paschal Aldrich owned a home on Buckeye Street that he shared with his wife, Martha. His home was also the first post office in the city.

When Dr. Aldrich died, Paschal inherited his large holdings, including a place on Coulee Road. Paschal then moved he and his family to Coulee Road, where he farmed for many years. Unfortunately, he took ill and had to sell much of the family's land. One account states that while Paschal was sick, his family lost their enormous holdings because of one man, who was never named.

While the man's identity may be a mystery, Paschal died on October 13, 1860. His wife, Martha, vowed to come back after her death as a ghost. Perhaps to persecute whoever had caused Paschal Aldrich's financial ruin? Could you blame her? After Pascal's death, family members and neighbors reported seeing him wandering the home, still looking after his family.

The small house, once a private residence, no longer stands; it is not known whether Pascal still roams the land he once farmed. Or if Martha has joined him.

City 21: Keshena

Menominee Casino Hotel

A surveillance camera at the hotel has picked up children running around in a restricted area of the hotel. When security checked to see why the children were there, the children had vanished from sight. They were, however, visible on camera.

The Menominee Casino Hotel is located at Highways 47/55 and Duquaine Road.

Menominee Tribal Police Department

Ghostly people wearing buckskin have been seen in the building, walking the hallways. At night the typewriter is said to type without the help of human fingers. Could this be attributed to the fact that the police department is built on an old Indian cemetery?

The Menominee Tribal Police Department is located at W3293 Wolf River Road.

City 22: Lac Du Flambeau

Bingo Hall

Pushy, pushy—that's how the ghost that is "felt" here is described. Workers there, as well as others, have experienced the feeling of being pushed by an invisible someone or something during the daytime hours.

Because this ghost hasn't made a one-time appearance and then vamoosed, some believe it is the ghost of a former patron of the hall, trying to get here or there. An elderly lady who used to push through people on her way to the bathroom is believed to be responsible for the current ghostly activity. She was said to be a very nice woman, but you know how it is—when you gotta go, you gotta go.

The sounds of a child talking and screaming have been reported by a surveillance man when he was alone at night. No one has any idea who this child could be. Some believe it is the residual haunting of a child who lived on the property years before the bingo hall was built.

City 23: Ladysmith

Cedar Lodge

Many believe that ghosts still belly up to the bar in this saloon. Customers—and lots of 'em—hear banging, strange lights, and extreme cold spots in the bar.

The saloon is located at N8004 Hwy 27. I've been told it serves up the best prime rib you'll ever sink your teeth into.

El Rancho Motel

Two words come to mind when many think of the motel: Bloody Bucket. This was the name of a bar that was located close to the location of the El Rancho—so goes the story attached this motel.

Now that I have your attention, I'll dive right into the story...er, two completely different stories about the haunting of the motel. One involves a murder stemming from a deal gone wrong that started at the Bloody Bucket, the other involves just plain unhappy spirits.

Let's start with the nicer story. The El Rancho, located at 8500 West Flambeau Avenue is said to rest on an old cemetery. The spirits said to haunt the motel are those of the dead in this built-upon cemetery. Cold spots are said to be proof of these unhappy cemetery campers.

The other story is a little more grizzly. And yes, it involves the Bloody Bucket—and some blood. The Bloody Bucket's bartender—mini tongue twister—told the owner that a customer wanted to talk to him in his nearby cattle barn about buying some cattle. The owner went to the barn, but was instead killed by a man with an axe. The murderer was never caught, but the bartender and the owner's wife got together shortly after and left town. Coincidence? I think not.

The ghost most associated with the El Rancho is a man in a red flannel shirt. This same ghost has been seen at a trailer court near the motel.

City 24: Land O' Lakes

Summerwind

This is one of the most notoriously haunted places in Wisconsin, even though it's now nothing more than ruins. Warning: If you do go to look for the ruins, get permission to be on the property. Otherwise, you'll be considered a trespasser and that's a big no-no.

The city of Land O' Lakes lies only a couple miles from the Wisconsin-Michigan border. Some say that flowers bloom on the site of the mansion during the night, but quickly close when the sun comes up. Others say the real haunting of the building was in the form of a woman ghost in white who used to dance in the dining room while the building was still standing.

The ruins of Summerwind lie on the shores of West Bay Lake. The mansion was built in 1916 by Robert P. Lamont, who would later go on to serve as the Secretary of Commerce under President Herbert Hoover. It was during this time that the mansion was rumored to harbor an evil spirit or two. One experience: The owner fired a gun at what he initially thought was an intruder. When the gunshot didn't produce a corpse, he changed his story to say the intruder was a resident ghost. Incredibly, Lamont kept the house. When he died, the house was sold. The ghost stories also died—until the 1970s.

That's when Arnold and Ginger Hinshaw and their six children moved to Summerwind. It's not known if they knew beforehand of the ghostly reputation of the estate, but it wasn't long before they began having ghostly experiences of their own. These experiences were in the form of shadows and shapes that flitted about the mansion, mumbled voices, and perhaps the most disturbing—the infamous ghostly shape of a woman floating in the dining room.

That would be enough to send most people packing, but this turned out to be just the beginning. Doors and windows would open on their own, and even raise and lower without the aid of human hands. Appliances would break down and then "fix" themselves before a repairman could be called. When the Hinshaws decided to renovate the historic house, workers refused to work there, claiming it was haunted. And once, when Mr. Hinshaw was on his way to his car, it suddenly burst into flames. Supernatural occurrence? Super nasty, if you ask me. But it gets worse.

Because no one would work for the Hinshaws, they had no choice but to do renovations themselves. It was during the painting of one room, that a human corpse was discovered in a hidden compartment.

Mr. Hinshaw, who had played the organ for enjoyment, began playing it as if possessed. And maybe he was. His raging sessions terrified the rest of the family. It wasn't long before Mr. Hinshaw had a breakdown of the mental variety. Then Mrs. Hinshaw was said to have attempted suicide. Mrs. Hinshaw and her children moved in with her parents. Long story short, she eventually divorced Mr. Hinshaw and remarried.

What happened next is so strange, it borders on incredible. The father of the former Mrs. Hinshaw, Raymond Bober, bought Summerwind—much to her horror and misery. Why, oh why, hadn't she told him about the awful things that had happened during her time there?

Though Bober agreed the house was haunted, he embraced the ghost. Bober claimed he knew who the ghost was and why it was at Summerwind. The ghost's name: Jonathan Carver, an eighteenth-century British explorer. Later Bober wrote a book about his experiences. He claimed rooms in the house would expand and shrink, items would disappear, and events that had happened at Summerwind years earlier seemed to replay themselves.

The stories of the mansion's fantastic past are intriguing. For now, that's all that remains of Summerwind. In 1988, the mansion was struck by lightning and burned to the ground.

Recent visitors to the site say they, too, have seen the legendary shadow men that walk the ruins. Who are these men? Former owners? Men from a time long before the mansion was built? Or are these men merely figments of one's overactive imagination stimulated by stories passed down from generation to generation?

City 25: Madeline Island

Sacrificial Hunger

I visited Madeline Island years ago to research historical information and learned about a small cemetery on the island that was believed to be haunted.

I recently learned these odd feelings may have something to do with the ghosts of Madeline Island. These spirits were said to roam the island long ago when it was heavily populated with Native Americans. So heavily populated that the men couldn't feed the population and a famine came to the island.

Now the bad part: Because there was no game or meat, the elders and medicine men of the tribe began sacrificing children and maidens. The people of Madeline Island survived this way until the people rebelled against the leaders and killed them.

The worst was over but tales of the spirits of the young maidens and children began spreading; they were dead, but they still lived as ghosts. There have been no recent reports of these particular Native American ghosts, but last century, sacrificial tobacco was found at the site of an ancient altar.

City 26: Manitowish Waters

Little Bohemia Lodge

With its rich history and link to the infamous John Dillinger, I would be surprised if this lodge near the shore of Little Star Lake wasn't haunted.

The story of John Dillinger and Little Bohemia begins just before April 20, 1934. Emil Wanatka was the then-owner of the Little Bohemia, and it just so happened that Wanatka and Dillinger shared the same legal counsel, Louis Piquett.

During that period in history, Dillinger was using several hideouts. For whatever reason, perhaps because Piquett was familiar to both Dillinger and Wanatka, Wanatka was offered $500 for three day's rent of the Little Bohemia. It is believed Piquett may have made some type of prearranged deal with Wanatka and then got it okayed by Dillinger. It's also likely Wanatka knew who Dillinger was, but business had been slow and Wanatka needed the money to pay his mortgage. Back then $500 was an awful lot of money. Wanatka would allow Dillinger and his entourage to stay there for three days. When Dillinger gave him the money, Wanatka's wife would then contact the FBI. It's worth mentioning that while $500 was a lot of money, a $10,000 reward on Dillinger's head was being offered at the same time.

On that fateful April afternoon in 1934, Dillinger's entourage began arriving at the Little Bohemia. Wanatka went out to greet Dillinger's gang. The men asked if they could have lunch and also if Wanatka could put up ten guests for a few days. The delighted proprietor fed the group and showed them to their rooms. One of the employees of the lodge who carried one of the bags commented that one of them felt as if it were filled with lead. Wanatka told him to mind his own business.

Dillinger and others, including Baby Face Nelson, arrived after five o'clock that afternoon. They had steak dinners, unpacked, and then checked out possible escape routes. There was only one possible exit for the group; not a good thing for a gang.

Later, Wanatka played poker with Dillinger and some of the others, but the stakes were too high and he had to bow out. At one point, he saw that Dillinger had two guns beneath his coat. Later, Wanatka looked through several newspapers and saw photos of Dillinger. That night, he and his wife tossed and turned. The sound of keys jingling, dogs barking, and constant footsteps on the stairs made them edgy; more so now that he knew without a doubt that he was harboring the notorious John Dillinger.

The next morning Wanatka confronted Dillinger and said he was a family man and didn't want any trouble. Dillinger assured him he and group only wanted to rest. Though Wanatka seemed trustworthy, Dillinger and his men kept a close eye on him.

Mrs. Wanatka asked permission to take Emil Jr. to a cousin's birthday party. The night before, she and Mr. Wanatka made a secret plan to rat out Dillinger. Dillinger, unaware that anything was amiss, agreed. It would turn out later that Baby Face Nelson, much more aware than Dillinger, followed Mrs. Wanatka. Let's just say that a lot of communication happened at the birthday party, and it wasn't just singing "Happy Birthday."

On April 23, 1934, just before the raid was to begin, Dillinger informed Wanatka that he was leaving early. On the other end, agents sent to Rhinelander found they only had one car. Things were beginning to unravel. Finally, the agents found transportation and arrived. They cut the headlights on their cars, put out their cigarettes, and walked to the lodge, wearing bulletproof vests. Unfortunately, as they approached, the Wanatkas' dogs began barking furiously. Three innocent guests left the building and drove away, only to be shot by FBI agents; one would die of his wounds. FBI agents then opened fire on the lodge, blasting everything in sight.

Dillinger and a couple of his men made a daring escape. That was the end of this story for a while—except for the hundreds of bullet holes in the lodge.

Dan Johns of the Little Bohemia Lodge confirmed the stories that the lodge is haunted. "Yes, people often talk about the lodge being haunted and most of the stories involve footsteps upstairs and unexplained noises in empty rooms. Also, I was told that an apparition has been seen in the windows on winter nights when the lodge was closed for the season."

C.G., a central Wisconsin preteen, recently stayed at Little Bohemia with her grandparents. "Grandma told me the lodge was haunted before we went there. At first I just thought it was just story. Then, at night, I heard it. I wasn't asleep yet. At first it sounded like someone walking past my bed to the window and then back to the front of the room. I heard it again later. It was really cool." She said her grandmother told her that she heard footsteps walk across the room that night, too.

Little Bohemia is a great place to stay, eat, or just soak up the incredible history. If you're lucky, you may just hear or see a ghost that may or may not be the famous John Dillinger.

You can find Little Bohemia at 142 Highway 51 South. And while you're there, you might want to try the Dillinger's Rockefeller or

John Dillinger's Signature Steak of Filet Medallions. I hear they are to die for.

City 27: Merrill

Scott Mansion

Big house, big ghost story. So big, that one Wisconsin tourism site even uses the word *haunted* to describe the mansion. Before I begin talking about the ghost or ghosts in the house, let me say that the house, in addition to being haunted, is also said to be cursed by an Indian Chief long before the mansion was built.

The ghost stories center on the tower. The ghost or ghosts that have been spotted catching a really great view from the top of the building are believed to be people strongly attached to the building.

T.B. Scott bought the land in 1884. He died unexpectedly in 1886, before the house could be built. Ann, his wife, died before another year

Scott Mansion, Merrill.

passed. Next, their son, Walter, was stabbed to death by the architect. The house was then sold in 1893, to a man who lost all his money and was forced to mortgage the house to a man named Tony Barsanti. Barsanti was stabbed to death in Chicago while waiting for a train to Merrill. Did I mention the house had a curse on it?

George Gibson bought the house in 1901, went to check it out, and was never seen again. Mary Fellhaber bought the house in 1906, and died soon after. But guess what—it doesn't end there. A caretaker died in 1912 after booking passage on the Titanic. Another caretaker died of alcoholism. The widower of Mary Fellhaber gave the property to the city in 1919, and the city then gave it to the Sisters of the Holy Cross. Generosity? Another reason perhaps?

For whatever reason, the final two acts of giving must have broken the curse. No more deaths have been associated with the house, although ghosts are routinely seen in the tower by residents and passersby.

I didn't see anything in the tower when I was there, but that doesn't mean they didn't see me.

The mansion is located on South Center Avenue next to the Good Samaritan Health Center. There are a couple of other really cool-to-look-at buildings between the house and the church.

Good Samaritan Health Center

The hospital, located at 601 South Center Avenue is said to be haunted.

The staff of the hospital, which is church-run, have seen ghosts in the old portion of the building.

There are also very cold spots in some halls in the old portion of the hospital.

City 28: Minoqua

Tula's Café

Minoqua is called one of the most naturally beautiful cities in Wisconsin. Is it any wonder ghosts hang around?

This particular ghost is said to belong to a man that died at the café. He's blamed for producing vaporous forms in the back hallway near the bathrooms where he was said to have met his demise.

Customers have noted cold spots in this restaurant-slash-coffee house, which is part of a strip mall. Employees of the café say things are not always as they were left when the café is opened the next day.

City 29: New Richmond

Kozy Korner

This is a great place to catch a bite and maybe a peek of the resident ghost, a boy named Carl. He may be a regular here, but he doesn't exactly make regular appearances. Some customers say in addition to seeing the boy, they've heard childish whispers nearby when there were no children there. Kozy Korner is located at 157 South Knowles Avenue.

City 30: Peshtigo

Peshtigo Fire Cemetery

On October 8, 1871, some 1,200 people lost their lives in what would be known as the inferno that caused the biggest loss of life in United States history. Even the Great Chicago Fire that happened at almost exactly at the same time (but got all the publicity), had a loss of life that was only a fraction of that suffered in Wisconsin.

Some experience rapid heartbeat and nausea at this site where 350 unidentified victims, some children, are buried. They attribute it to the intense emotion of thinking about those that perished in the fire. Others feel a rush of cold air outdoors on warm days.

The mass grave is located on Oconto Avenue. An historical marker was erected in 1951, but the ghosts of the Peshtigo Fire have been here for more than a hundred years.

Other ghosts near Peshtigo have been seen. These include four little girl ghosts in singed nightgowns, a ghost whose charred body you can smell, a burning Indian village, and a caravan of burning wagons.

City 31: Phillips

Elk Lake Dam

The ghost who haunts the Elk Lake Dam is called Mary for the young woman who was murdered here. Mary's ghost has been seen numerous times walking near the water's edge and also on the dam itself.

The young hitchhiker was killed in February, 1974, and her murder has never been solved. Some residents of the town believe the attacker lives nearby.

One woman who lives near the dam claims that a young woman named Mary repeatedly walked from the river and visited her.

Fishermen have seen white shapes behind them and heard odd noises when no one was around. Some say it's just Mary, trying to get your attention.

City 32: Rhinelander

Pine Lake Road

Urban legend? Verifiable haunting? You be the judge. The story starts with Molly. In one story, she's a girl. In another story, she's a young woman. As a woman, Molly was said to have died when she crashed her car into a huge rock on Pine Lake Road. In the young girl version of the story, Molly was from Chicago and used to visit the rock each summer. Visit a rock? Must be a Chicago thing. And what happened to young Molly that the rock became haunted?

So many questions—so few answers. One thing locals agree upon is that the rock is haunted. If someone should sit on Molly's rock, they will get shoved off. Not only that, they will hear an accompanying warning, "Get off my rock!"

People came from afar to see this talking haunted rock. Hundreds, maybe even thousands of people came to see Molly's rock. The city and county blew up the rock to stop the flood of people to Pine Lake Road. There's now an indentation where the rock used to be, near the intersection of Pine Lake Road and Highway D.

Did this make Molly angry? Duh. Of course it did. So angry that the ghost cursed all the pieces of rock. It's said that if you pick up a piece of Molly's rock and take it with you, you'll be cursed/haunted until you bring it back where it belongs.

Others that drive by the spot where the rock used to be say they see a elliptical light that looks like halo. The story of Molly's Rock on Pine Lake Road is known throughout the state.

St. Joseph's and St. Mary's Catholic Cemetery

Known more simply as St. Joseph's or St. Joe's Cemetery, this is one cemetery you might want to avoid when you're alone or with someone who likes to play practical jokes. Those who visit the cemetery say they often hear whispering when no one is around.

St. Joseph's and St. Mary's Catholic Cemetery is located on Lincoln Street.

City 33: Rib Lake

Rib Lake Lakeview Campground

Everyone likes to hear a scary story around a campfire. Not so much if there just happens to be a ghost right next door to where you're camping, who might be listening in.

The Rib Lake Lakeview Campground is said be haunted by a ghost or ghosts from the nearby cemetery. Some say a young boy who is buried next door at the aptly named Lake View Cemetery is responsible for the unearthly noises that can heard on quiet nights.

City 34: Rothschild

Fischer House

What took place at this house—I'm talking *scaaaaaaaary*—is said to be the basis for the movie *Poltergeist*.

The ghost, said to be a poltergeist because of the way it terrorized its victims, resided at a home belonging to the Fischer family in the 1970s. The sound of ringing bells and footsteps with no one attached to them could be heard in the home. Spontaneous fires occurred along with unexplained electrical malfunctions; doors opened and closed on their own.

Those taking a bath at the home never knew what to expect. You could have hot water in the tub one moment and it would be icy cold the next. The family dog refused to go into certain places of the home—can you blame it?

In addition to the above, odd shadows were often seen moving along the wall. But by far the worst activity in this insanely haunted house, was a razor attacking Mrs. Fischer when she was taking a bath.

The Fischers moved out after this occurrence. Some believe the home had so many paranormal occurrences because it was built on a Native American burial ground. The home is currently not believed to be haunted. If it is, no one's talking.

House on Woodward Avenue

This house on Woodward Avenue in Rothschild has been described as haunted as recently as 2003. At that time, a woman's preteen daughter was lying in bed when a little girl crawled in bed with her.

Thinking it was her little sister, the preteen awoke. On her way past her sister's room, she saw her little sister sleeping soundly, wearing different clothes. When she returned to her room, the differently dressed little girl had disappeared.

The human children's mother also saw the ghost child when she was alone in the house. She didn't see the child as clearly as her daughter did, but she still saw her. The ghostly girl didn't harm anyone, but her presence was said to be "disturbing."

Things go missing in this house only to be found somewhere else. The house is located on the 900 block of Woodward.

City 35: Spooner

Corral Bar

The female ghost said to haunt this bar isn't very happy. Maybe it's because she was murdered when she was a bartender there decades ago. She was found tossed in a corner.

She is said to be responsible for wreaking havoc with the jukebox; she doesn't play one song, she likes them all and goes through them so fast you can barely guess what's playing before the next one is up.

The woman's murderer wasn't caught right away, but eventually was apprehended when he committed another murder. Many have seen the ghost's reflection in the mirror from a corner of the bar. She's also been seen as a shadow making her way across the room.

The bar is located at 114 Walnut Street, just off Highway 63.

Hammill House

Known as the "Father of Spooner," Frank Hammill, is said to haunt this incredible mansion, which also happens to be the first stop on the Spooner Heritage Tour.

Spooner was a well-respected railroad man, mayor, and state legislator who died in 1922 of a mysterious stomach illness. After he died, his body was displayed in the house.

Spooner's wife lived in the house until she died and was said to feel her husband's presence there. Subsequent owners report feeling Frank's presence, too.

Throughout the years, Hammill says *hello* in a number of ways including footsteps, voices, and the feeling that someone is right behind you.

City 36: Superior

Fairlawn Mansion and Museum

This beautiful mansion is located at 906 East 2nd Street and is huge—forty-two rooms to be exact. It was completed in 1891, at the cost of $150,000, and was featured on the A&E Network as one of *America's Castles*.

It was built by three-time mayor of Superior, Martin Pattison, and commands an incredible view of the bay and Lake Superior. He shared the mansion with his wife, Gracie, and their six children. When Pattison died in 1918, Grace Pattison donated the mansion. It then became the Superior Children's Home and Refuge and served more than 2,000 children over the course of forty-two years.

One ghost that seems to be a permanent resident of the mansion is that of a "guide" that helps visitors find their way around and then disappears. Some believe it is a former maid who was murdered by her husband. She didn't die at the mansion, but apparently loved Fairlawn and the Pattisons so much that she decided to make it her eternal home. She has been seen many times on the stairway near the second floor.

Other ghosts that have been seen on the property are said to be the ghosts of children who stayed here when it was a home for children and unwed mothers. Though no children are believed to have died on the property, no one can be 100 percent certain because records have been sealed.

The sounds of children playing near the basement pool are a common sound. Two little girl ghosts have been spotted here numerous times.

City 37: Tomahawk

Bootleggers Supper Club

This popular eatery is located at 2001 Indian Pine Point Road on Lake Nokomis. Built in 1928, the supper club with a 1920s atmosphere was a popular hangout for gangsters of the time including Capone and Dillinger. Back then it was known as Phil's Resort and Phil's Place.

Customers say the food, servers, and atmosphere can't be beat. Employees, renters, and others say there's also a lot of ghostly activity going on in the background.

The basement area is a place that gives many a very uneasy feeling, despite the fact, there's nothing you can see that would make you feel that way.

One upstairs apartment renter said her well-adjusted daughter refused to sleep alone. The girl was only happy if she could jump in bed with her mother. Finally, the mother asked her why. The little girl said there was a lady in her room. Sure enough. The renter went in the room one day and saw a woman in a white dress in her daughter's bedroom. They moved out very shortly after.

This same woman has been seen walking through the dining room after she has come down from upstairs.

Two other renters couldn't sleep upstairs, either. But it wasn't a woman in a white dress; it was the sound of constant pacing, believed to be caused by the ghost of Phil, the former owner.

The ghosts seem quite content where they are. So content, that one bartender even saw a woman ghost sitting at his feet. Clear-as-a-bell laughter has also been heard in the establishment.

A baby monitor in an apartment picked up the sound of a woman and child talking in the baby's room, though no woman or child had been there. The jury is out on whether this occurrence should be categorized as sweet or creepy.

And that's not all: The apparition of a woman in an upstairs window when the area was gutted out has been seen.

When the guests at the bar feel a cold blast of air, they think it's "cool" because they know it's probably just Phil, checking on the guests at the supper club to make sure they're happy.

City 38: Townsend

Hillcrest Lodge

Karla and Jim Schuessler have seen and heard things in this more than sixty-year-old building that defy logical explanation. However, these occurrences can be explained quite nicely if you attribute them to a former third-floor resident of the lodge named Dr. Fred.

Shortly after Dr. Fred was killed, while walking on County Road T near the lodge, odd things began happening. Karla remembers one incident like it was yesterday. She and her husband, Jim, were living upstairs in the living quarters while they were building a new home. It was a Sunday night and she was shutting the lodge down for the night. "I dropped a roll of quarters," she says. "I picked them all up and then walked away. When I came back, I found a quarter on the floor. Thinking I must have missed one, I put it in the till."

That should have been the end of the story, but of course it wasn't. Karla continued shutting down. As she walked past the till, she found *another* quarter on the floor. Strange? Maybe not. "Dr. Fred was said to have a fascination with coins," she says.

That same night she went behind the bar and found the beer tap was wide open and beer was all over the floor. One may chalk this up to being tired and not closing the tap properly, but it isn't so easy to explain other things that have happened.

Karla says there's one weird window in the lodge that was put in upside down. "It locks up instead of down. I locked the window and walked away. When I came back, the window was unlocked and open."

She says she and Jim had another experience where they heard what sounded like a ball dropping on the floor. The building has hardwood floors and they're used to the sound of creaking, but this sound was unlike anything they had ever heard. Suddenly, the loud sound of something rolling made them pause, but it didn't sound like a ball; it sounded like an office chair rolling across the floor. Jim wanted to investigate, but Karla declined. "Oh, no. We're staying right here!" she told him.

Another strange thing that happened here in previous years: The CD jukebox has gone into random play only to play "your" song.

The lodge is located at 16704 Nicolet Road with a great view of the Townsend Flowage. The food is excellent, too.

City 39: Washington Island

Nelsen's Hall Bitters Pub

This pub has two claims to fame. One is being the oldest continuous operating tavern in the state of Wisconsin: It was built in 1899 by Danish immigrant, Tom Nelson. The other is for being super haunted.

Er…make that three claims to fame: According to the Guinness Book of World Records, Nelsen's Hall Bitters Pub is the single largest seller of Angostura Bitters in the world. Yep, the world.

Tom Nelsen had a custom of drinking Angostura Bitters as a stomach tonic throughout most of his life. He drank a lot of it—nearly a pint a day. Even when Prohibition prohibited other taverns from selling alcohol, Tom Nelsen applied for a license as a pharmacist and was able to sell the ninety-proof "tonic" in his saloon during Prohibition. Looks like we're up to four claims to fame: More than 10,000 people each and every year down a shot of bitters. This entitles them to become a card-carrying member of the Bitters Club, issued by Nelsen's Hall.

There are stories of encounters with a ghost in a restroom here. Objects have also been known to wander around on their own, and an employee was tapped on the back while building shelves in the hand-dug basement. He was alone.

Even today, the ghost of former owner, Tom Nelsen, makes sure his customers are well taken care of. The pub is located at 1201 Main Street.

Porte des Morte

The passageway between Washington Island and Door County was called Porte des Morte, or Death's Door, by the early French explorers. No reason in particular, but it could be because of the way those in canoes, boats, and ships didn't always reach their destination if Porte des Morte happened to be on their route.

Phantom ship alert! One might not expect to see a phantom ship near such a populated area like Green Bay, but hey, phantom ships pretty much do what they please.

The phantom ship I'm talking about was named *Le Griffon*. She belonged to the famous, if a bit destitute, French explorer, René Robert Cavelier, Sieur de La Salle. (Even saying the name without an accent, it sounds fancy!) On a hot summer day in 1679, La Salle docked *Le Griffon* on Washington Island. He then took a canoe trip down the St. Joseph River. His purpose: to look for a water link to the Mississippi River.

About five weeks later, the explorer's ship headed back to Niagara without him. It was never seen again, at least not in solid form. This was because *Le Griffon* was wrecked in Canada—most likely through the treachery of creditors.

But like other ghosts, *Le Griffon*, doesn't realize she is gone. She has been seen often since then, as a phantom ship in the fog of Green Bay Harbor.

Range Line Road

This ghost story is mentioned a lot, but there aren't a lot of details. It goes like this: There's a milkmaid, she's very tall, she's a ghost, her name is Gretchen, and she's been spotted walking along Range Line Road.

And get this: Sometimes she has no legs! Range Line Road touches County W to the north and County W to the south.

City 40: Wausau

The Fillmor

This building, located at 310 North 4th Street, was once Roger's Cinema. When this building was Roger's Cinema it had a long history of being inhabited by a ghostly presence.

The Fillmor, Wausau.

The original building was constructed in the early twentieth century as a retail center. Not long after, in the mid-1920s, a funeral home opened in the building and stayed there for about fifteen years. In 1945, the Hollywood Theatre was established on the ground floor. Later, it operated under the name Roger's Cinema. It was still Roger's Cinema when it ceased operations as a theater.

The basement auditorium was where much of the paranormal phenomenon associated with the site was said to take place. Many former employees witnessed lights flipping on and off by themselves, projectors shutting off during showings, and other electrical anomalies. They attributed this to a spirit they named Bob. One employee was pushed by invisible hands through theater doors. But perhaps the most unnerving occurrence has to do with the theater chairs themselves.

Employees reported empty seats rocking, as if guests of the theater had just gotten out of them (when no one had). Most believed a former stage manager was responsible. Worse, employees and other witnesses sometimes watched rows of chairs rock by themselves. And renovators who were working on the building after it closed heard thumping, looked up, and saw every chair in the building rocking violently back and forth.

Another possible identity for the ghostly presence: A prostitute was rumored to have been killed in the building in the early days of its existence.

The Fillmor, now open for business, has a newly remodeled interior and great entertainment. What it doesn't have—at least according to an employee I asked—is ghosts. "At least none that I've seen," the employee told me. "But I've heard rumors, so it wouldn't surprise me."

Grand Theater

This building, located at 401 North 4th Street, was built in 1927 to replace the old Grand Opera House. Though the building, inside and out, is very easy on the eyes, you would have a hard time finding someone who lives in Wausau who believes the Grand isn't haunted. Its goose-bump-inducing reputation as a house for a ghost or two began way back in the 1950s. Film canisters would move from one place to another. Then the strangeness progressed to cold spots, the feeling that someone was watching you, and finally, in your face, "look what I can do" antics.

Investigations have turned up paranormal activity including a mysterious blob in the balcony, film of a blob of light moving

Grand Theater, Wausau.

across a room, a ball of light, and an EVP of a ghostly voice issuing a warning.

Others have felt cold drafts, captured orbs in photos, and have seen a ghostly man making his way down the staircase or along the back wall of the balcony.

Today, strange goings-on continue to go on. A ghost named Larry is said to regularly watch rehearsals from the wings; he's seen most often in the stage area. One human man said he's heard footsteps walk past him when he was alone.

Haunted Hangar

In the 1940s, Archie, the airport manager, was said to have died in a crash at the airport. Apparently, no one ever told him. Witnesses have reported hearing ghostly footsteps. The plumbing in the building is not immune to ghostly tinkering, either. Archie is said to be responsible for turning on a water faucet and leaving it on.

During the latest round of renovations, ghostly activity was said to have increased. The Wausau Municipal Airport is located at 725 Woods Place.

Landmark Apartments

Ghosts like the Landmark—at least that's what the tenants, past and present, say. One former renter said that was the reason he rented here a couple years back—he was hoping to share his apartment with a ghost. Unfortunately for him, his apartment was ghost-free.

How do the apartment dwellers of the Landmark, located at 221 Scott Street in downtown Wausau, know they have ghosts in residence? Reports of unexplained creaking, knocking on doors (and there's no one there to do the knocking), and fickle lights have convinced residents they're not alone. What would you think if you turned off the lights, they went back on, you turned them off, and they went back on? Oh, and you saw the switch move by itself? Faulty wiring...or a ghost? And that's not all. More than one renter has admitted feeling the cool brush of an invisible passerby when walking up the stairs.

Marathon County Historical Museum

Like many old mansions with a rich history, this aged abode is said to be haunted. The museum, also known as the Yawkey Mansion,

Landmark Apartments, Wausau.

is located at 403 McIndoe and was built in 1900 or 1901 by Cyrus C. Yawkey. He died in 1943, but his wife, Alice, lived there until she died in 1953. Their daughter, Leigh Yawkey Woodson, later donated the house to the Marathon County Historical Society.

A museum curator reportedly opened the museum one day and found items on the floor in Mr. Yawkey's old office area that had been moved from other areas. A book of poetry also seems to have been manipulated by ghostly hands; it moved out of one exhibit completely.

Employees have also witnessed a pop bottle cap moving across a table on its own. One employee heard his name called when he was alone; when he tried to leave the basement, he had to struggle to exit the door because it was held shut by invisible hands.

Visitors sometimes get a whiff of pipe smoke on the first-floor staircase landing, though no one earthly is smoking.

Marathon County Historical Museum, Wausau.

Marathon County Historical Society Administration Building, Wausau.

Marathon County Historical Society

Administration Building

The building, located at 410 McIndoe, is the former A.P. Woodson House. The ghost said to haunt the building likes his or her exercise. The sound of footsteps can be heard making their way from an upstairs hallway, down the stairs to the first floor. Maybe the ghost is leaving the upstairs because of a strange odor that is said to come from the upstairs.

One of the coolest—in my opinion—signs the building is truly haunted, is the sound of a phone ringing in a room that doesn't have a phone. In addition to the ringing phone, the door alarm is said to go off for no earthly reason.

Shepherd & Schaller Sporting Goods

Ed is believed to be the ghost in residence at this historic building in downtown Wausau. He is said to rap on doors and walls and also set off door alarms. Other strange events include lights turning off and on in

Shepherd & Schaller Sporting Goods, Wausau.

the upstairs storeroom, and items disappearing and then reappearing in totally different places.

One worker had a piece of plaster leave a wall and fly at her as she was walking to the attic. A hint that she shouldn't go up there?

JC Penney once had a store at this location and Ed is believed to the name of one of the custodians. He is said to be a friendly presence, though the flying plaster makes one wonder.

The sporting goods store is located at 324 Scott Street.

Stone Crest Residence and Forest Park Village

Forest Park Village was formerly Old Hospital North until the 1980s. During the time before it was abandoned and renovated into a home for the elderly, the former morgue was said to be a gathering place for cultists.

People often saw shadows and disembodied voices coming from the dilapidated building. Even after the cultists were arrested and the building was renovated, the haunting of the building continued. Today, the sounds of ghostly children can be heard. If you happen to take the elevator, you might want to check first for ghostly passengers—they've been reported hitching a ride. Like many big old buildings, there are many places where cold spots are felt. Many who travel the halls say they are assailed with feelings of unease in certain spots.

Stone Crest Residence, another home for the elderly is located at 805 Parcher Street. While it doesn't have the cult history of Forest Park Village, it does have a reputation as being haunted. Some have reported seeing children peering outside the windows of the building in the evening hours.

UW—Marathon County

This two-year liberal arts college is known for not one ghost, but two. The first ghost, Annie, is the most well-known to students and staff. She's said to be responsible for the sound of moving furniture in empty classrooms, specifically the sound of wooden chairs being dragged across the floor. No, she isn't a compulsive re-arranger; she was a janitor. In life and in death, she's known for her distinctive laugh, something else that has been heard coming from various parts of the school.

The good-natured former janitor, who used to join other members of the custodial staff before their morning shift for coffee, has also been blamed for opening all the cupboard doors in the library workroom. Custodians on the late shift have also heard footsteps in the hallway above the maintenance office and break room. The well-liked Annie, known for her chicken-like cackle, died of throat cancer. In the afterlife, she appears to be illness free and as happy as she was when she worked at the university.

The other ghost is called the Blue Cowboy, mostly because of the cowboy hat that is a part of the hazy blue apparition that appears in the closet of a third-floor room. So he's a closet cowboy? The Blue Cowboy, once he makes his appearance, is said to mosey down the hall. When residents of the room are out of town for the weekend, they sometimes return to find their furniture has been moved.

The university is located at 518 South 7th Avenue.

The Wausau Club

Until it closed in 2004, the Wausau Club located at 309 McClellan Street was a playground for Martha, the resident ghost. She was said to be responsible for a host of ghostly activity including tossing dishes, swinging the chandelier, flipping light switches back on, and making appearances on the grand staircase—a grand sight, no doubt. Martha was also spotted in the north-room doorway.

Martha was believed to have been a guest at the stately club when it was first built. She was said to have been heartbroken and ended her life there.

The building is currently being renovated and Martha is believed to still be in residence. Tools and equipment never stay where workers leave them. Does this mean Martha wants them to go away, or that she wants them to work where she leaves the tools?

The building was built in 1865; it is listed in the U.S. National Register of Historic Places.

City 4: Zoar

State Highway 47

An old Indian cemetery on Highway 47 that lies between the cities of Phlox and Neopit is said to be haunted. Heck, some say the entire area around the cemetery is haunted. If you're in the vicinity, a ghostly presence is said to do strange things to your vehicle.

Your car might stall for no reason. Or, if you happen to be driving by at night, your lights may say night-night. Those that have experienced this say they drive away as fast as safety allows until their lights miraculously come back on again.

Oh, and don't be alarmed if you happen to see a man with no face walking down the highway away from the cemetery. This ghost is not a Native American, however, so it's likely his grave is somewhere else.

One person I spoke to said this ghost belongs to a man who was killed in a motorcycle accident near the location of his cemetery.

2

Central Wisconsin Ghosts

Adams County

Karen's Ghosts

Karen Rathke, formerly of Adams County, has had a number of ghostly encounters during her life. The nice thing: Most of these encounters were reassuring, happy ones.

Her first encounter happened when she was a young girl. "When I was about nine, my grandpa died. I was very close to him so I took his death very hard."

She says he died in his bed, an old horsehair mattress that she wishes she had now. "My mom moved his bed to another room, as my sister and I had shared a room."

Rathke says she comes from a family with a weird sense of humor. "I can still remember this as clear as can be. I woke up one morning to birds singing and my [deceased] grandpa standing in the doorway, laughing." She says he spoke to her then and said, "What are you doing sleeping in my bed?" in the same tone as the "Three Bears" story.

The next time Rathke had a encounter was when she lived on Cypress Drive in Friendship. She had a weird "dream" one morning that her mother had died. She went to see her mother and told her about the dream. As Rathke left, her mother's last words to her were, "You and that damn dream."

The next day, Rathke asked her husband to call the hospital about two minutes before the hospital called to tell her come there immediately. Rathke's mother died before Rathke got there.

Rathke told me, "My mom and I used to walk daily. After her death, as I was walking alone and thinking of her and missing her, I felt a hand in the small of my back." She believes it was her mother's way of comforting her from beyond.

Years later, another member of Rathke's family died. "When our brother-in-law, Ed, died, the guys were cleaning the cottage for my sister and forgot one refrigerator. They went back in and a rainbow was shining upon it."

K. L. Rathke and husband, Don. *Courtesy of K. L. and Don Rathke.*

At Ed's graveside service, a sundog appeared. "One day, driving on County Z, I was telling my husband, Don, if you only had a sign that Ed was at peace, it would help. At that instant, a sundog appeared over the water."

Another interesting experience: Rathke and her husband rented a house from an aunt. They could always smell peppermint. They questioned the aunt, who told them that her dead mother's favorite candy was peppermint.

But Rathke's experiences aren't always linked to her family. When she first moved to Lake Camelot in Adams County, Rathke saw a ghostly young man at a beach club pier. She questioned a neighbor, who said a young man drowned off the pier years before.

Rathke currently lives in Arizona with her husband, Don. So far she hasn't had any ghostly experiences in her new home.

City 43: Almond

Spiritland Cemetery

This country cemetery located between Almond and Plainfield at the intersections of County D and BB has long been rumored to be the final resting place of Ed Gein. It is not. He is buried elsewhere and his grave is not marked to prevent vandalism.

Spiritland Cemetery, Almond

However, a former coworker told me that when he was a young child staying at his grandmother's house adjacent to the cemetery, he used to see a man digging up bodies in the cemetery. When he told his grandmother about it, she waved his story away, by telling him he was seeing a ghost!

Many years later, it was revealed that the *ghost* my former coworker saw was really Ed Gein, who is believed to have dug up at least one body there.

The ghost said to haunt the Spiritland, oddly enough, isn't associated with the restless soul of one of the unfortunate bodies believed to have been dug up by the ghoulish Gein.

The spirit that haunts Spiritland is said to be that of a man who often visited his wife's grave there when he was alive. The man, Dewitt McLaughlin, was one of Almond's earliest settlers. McLaughlin claimed that while he was at the cemetery visiting his dead wife, her spirit would visit him.

I visited the cemetery. For some reason, I was immediately drawn to the headstones belonging to Mr. and Mrs. McLaughlin. Unfortunately, the dates on the stones don't support the story. Dewitt McLaughlin lived from 1864 to 1925. Jessie McLaughlin lived from 1865 to 1935. Jessie survived Dewitt by ten years. She would have had to have seen his spirit, not the other way around.

City 44: Appleton

Appleton Curling Club

Established in 1939, this building certainly doesn't look menacing... or hint that it is a habitat for paranormal activity. But looks, as we all know, can be deceiving.

Ghostly footsteps can be heard in the upstairs areas of the club, and not hit and miss. The sound of paranormal pitter-patter is heard on a regular basis.

People at the club have also been privy to apparitions of old—and dead—club members. Sometimes, noises such as "clopping" and "whooshing" accompany these apparitions.

A former club member is said to be responsible for knocking over chairs and glasses in the pub, and many have reported smelling cigar smoke even when no one is or has been smoking.

It would seem that a favorite hangout is a favorite hangout, whether you're living or not.

Appleton Curling Club, Appleton

Dairy Queen, Appleton.

Diary Queen

This building looks like a nice, typical new-ish Dairy Queen. Because it's said to be haunted, you might first assume that something bad happened inside or just outside the building. You would be wrong. Nothing bad has happened inside or out of the building since the Dairy Queen was built.

It's believed the presence that has taken up ghostly residence is attached to the bar that once stood where the Dairy Queen is now.

The ghost isn't what one would call menacing, but workers here say the they've experienced too many weird things to chalk it up to coincidence. Among the things workers have heard: odd noises such as the sound of shuffling feet, someone clearing their throat, and coins clinking together. Lights shut off at times for no reason, and cold drafts have been felt nowhere near any ice cream.

I couldn't find any live bodies that would admit seeing or feeling a ghostly presence when I visited the site. But that doesn't mean there aren't any.

The Dairy Queen is located at 1813 North Richmond Street.

Fox River Mills Apartments

This former paper mill, now a gigantic rental complex, is eye catching because of its sheer size. It's also haunted—at least according to current and former residents.

Fox River Mills Apartments, Appleton.

One former resident says she was in her apartment and lying on her side on her futon in the living room when she heard whispering in her ear. She says she was half asleep at the time, but when the whispering started, it instantly woke her. She, of course, looked around, but no one was there. This happened several more times before she moved out.

Another time, she was on her computer, editing photos in her Web cam software. The cam was on and she had it pointing at the wall. She says, "Well, I just happened to look over at the cam screen on the computer and there was a gray outline of a face that flashed on and then off. It was odd." She also has a video on her computer of her mouse just moving randomly all over the screen.

A current resident, who also didn't want to be named, said he and guests have heard someone—an invisible someone—walk past them when they're inside his apartment. He's also felt a cold breeze wrap around him when the windows and doors have been closed and no air conditioning has been on.

Sometimes, he can hear yelling right next to him when no one is there. He has no idea who the yeller is, just that he or she is very annoying.

Multi-level apartments and townhouses on the Fox River.

The Fox River Mills Apartments complex is located on East Water Street.

You can't miss it.

Hearthstone House

If this house is haunted now, when did it happen? Priscilla, a friend of mine, said her mother used to play here when she was a young child (in between owners). She said her mother and her friends would crawl in through the windows of this incredible home, but if there was a mention of the home being haunted, she doesn't remember it.

Today, many people believe this house is haunted; everyone agrees it's unique. Hearthstone, located at 625 W. Prospect Avenue, has bragging rights to being the world's (yes, I said world's) first home to be lighted by a central hydroelectric station. This event happened way back in 1882, September 30th to be exact. Back then it was owned by a paper company exec and banker named Henry James Rogers. Rogers is not believed to be the Hearthstone's haunter.

A.W. Priest, a former owner who bought the house in 1900, is the ghost said to keep coming back to this well-heeled address, now a

Hearthstone House, Appleton.

museum. Volunteers have said they feel someone watching them—and not in a nice way. They've said his presence has a disapproving feel to it.

Many unexplained sounds have been heard here, including sneezing when no one is there. Perhaps Mr. Priest has an allergy to the present?

But not all of those who experience this otherworldly presence find it off-putting. An office manager was said to greet the ghost every morning when she opened for the day by saying, "Good morning, Mr. Priest."

There are others who also could be responsible for the ghostly presence. One is John G. Badenoch, who used the house as a restaurant. No word if then-diners got an eyeful of ghost with their dinner. The restaurant switched hands in 1933, when Badenoch handed the rental reins over to Frank Harriman. The restaurant closed in 1938, and two years later the house was sold to Frederick H. Hoffman.

In 1986, the Friends of Hearthstone Inc. bought the house. Two years later, it opened as a museum.

When I called the Hearthstone, the lady on the other end of the line told me nicely, but emphatically, that the Hearthstone is not haunted. Ghosts or not, the Hearthstone is a very cool building to tour.

Huntley Elementary School

Here's an usual ghost story. The haunting said to take place in the vicinity of the school started in the late 1920s—the glory days of the Mob. During those days, a young man named Marky was said to be associated with the Mob. The unusual element of the story is that the color purple is mentioned along with Marky. Sometimes it's linked to Marky's demise, some say he had a premonition about the color leading to his death, and others say he just plain didn't like the color purple. Regardless, he was said to be prone to fits, and when he had these fits, the color purple is always mentioned.

Moving right along... After Marky died (how is a mystery), he was sometimes spotted conversing with others his age outside the school. That is, until they realized they were living and he was dead.

To this day, he's been spotted throwing fits in the area of the school. This takes place at night. I couldn't find any information on where Marky grew up, but it's said he still haunts the home.

When I visited the school during the daytime, I saw nothing out of the ordinary, didn't get any bad vibes, nor did I have trouble with my camera. Still, I was waiting for him to strike up a conversation—or a fit—for me.

Pilot's House

One Appleton pilot lives in a haunted house—at least that's what some believe. He says, "My house was built in the 1930s and both my girlfriend and brother have feelings that there has been ghostly activity here. For me, I don't think too much of it, but sometimes I say 'hi' and feel that if something does exist, it is of a friendly nature."

He says his brother swore that when he lived in the home with him, there was a box that mysteriously came out of the closet on its own and became damp on the bottom. It ended up staining the carpet and in the process, making the pilot a little angry. At the time, the pilot thought his brother might have been drunk and did it himself. Now he wonders.

When the pilot was a kid, he used to visit his grandmother's house in Buffalo, New York. In that old house they experienced ghostly occurrences to the point where they finally called paranormal experts to come in to see if there was anything going on. He remembers the cassette recording of paranormal activity that he heard when he visited there with his older brothers. He remembers this as being strange and scary.

He isn't sure if his elderly grandmother still has the cassette, but he remembers what was on it. "It was creepy," he remembers. Maybe end with a Sherryism: It's been documented in many cases, that if

63

a person is open to a haunting in one place, that the paranormal will be evident in other places for that person if present. That just may be the case in Appleton for our pilot—or has the ghost flown the coup.

Riverside Cemetery

I toured the cemetery on a muddy, unseasonably warm day. The cemetery, for the most part, didn't make me want to beat a hasty retreat, and my camera didn't issue any strange photos. There was one place near the river's edge, though, that made me feel odd, for lack of a better word.

I never did find Kate Blood's tombstone—the reason this cemetery is supposed to be haunted. The rationale behind this tombstone being talked about: It's said to ooze a blood-like substance. There are a number of other stories that go along with the cluster of tombstones here, but nothing that can be substantiated.

The sound of ghostly howling is another feature of this cemetery located at 714 North Owaissa Street.

Secura Insurance Companies

Some say the area at the rear of the building is haunted by the ghost of a little girl who drowned here more than a hundred and fifty years ago while picnicking with her parents. Her parents are also said to haunt this pond area. The story: She fell into a pond on the property and got stuck in a pipe and drowned. This is where things get a little confusing.

There is a pond on the property, a beautiful pond no matter what season it is, but it isn't located in the area where the little girl is said to have drowned. Nevertheless, many say they've heard the faint, blood-chilling screams of adults and a child near the current location of the pond.

City 45: Arpin

Powers Bluff

This popular recreation area, also called Skunk Hill, is located at 6990 Bluff Drive. Native Americans have been attached to the bluff for centuries. In the 1800s, the Potawatomi Indians who lived on Skunk Hill held ceremonial dances that brought many other different tribes to the area.

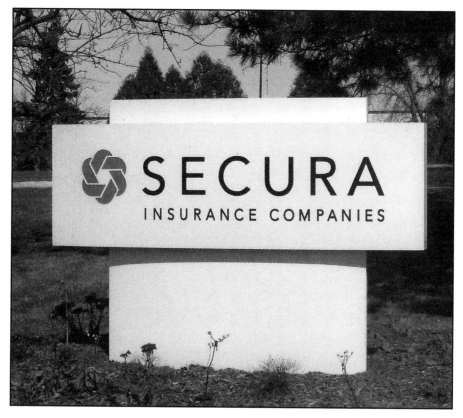

Secura Insurance Companies, Appleton.

The place here said to be the most haunted is a rock that protrudes from the top of the hill. This rock is called "Spirit's Chair." Also on the hill—a rather large cemetery that is the final earthly resting place of many famous Native American warriors. This cemetery is one of two here; one at the top and one at the bottom. Che-chaw-kose, who was mentioned in the Treaty of October 27, 1832, made at Tippecanoe River, is said to be buried in one of them.

Five mounds, located about three-quarters of a mile east of Skunk Hill are also believed to be haunted. These mounds are known as the Grimm Mound Group because of the farm where they are located. Three skeletons were found in one of the mounds. This area, like Skunk Hill, is a village and cemetery site.

You don't have to be Native American to feel the spiritual Native American presence. Visitors to the park often express feelings of sadness or of being overwhelmed. Gusts of wind on an otherwise calm day are sometimes felt in the area of the Spirit's Chair.

City 46: Baileys Harbor

Cana Island Lighthouse

Cana Island Lighthouse is located north of Baileys Harbor, off County Highway Q. This particular lighthouse is not believed to be haunted, but the grounds around the lighthouse are. Lighthouse keepers began tending to the light way back in 1869. I couldn't find any records of a lighthouse keeper dying here, but a man is rumored to have drowned in the area back in the 1930s.

This man said to haunt the island, especially near the lighthouse, makes himself known by making appearances as a white, moving shape.

FYI, you can actually walk across the rock causeway from the Door County mainland right straight to Cana Island. How cool is that?

City 47: Bowler

Bowler High School and Bowler Middle School

This small combined school located at 500 South Almon Road is the site of several different types of paranormal activity.

Young children have been heard and seen running down the halls of the school. High school students have heard small children crying and witnessed their lockers opening and closing on their own. Some have had their books inexplicably fly out of their hands.

Predawn visits to the school are times when some have heard the sound of slamming doors on the inside of the school in rooms that are unlit and unoccupied.

City 48: Caryville

Caryville Cemetery

This cemetery, also known as Sand Hill Cemetery is located on Frostbrook Road. This very small cemetery with less than two dozen graves sits on the top of a hill north of Caryville off County H. This overgrown final resting place is very difficult to find, mainly because of the way the roads are marked.

Ghostly children have been seen in the vicinity of the cemetery, some playing in the nearby cornfields. Other witnesses have claimed to see children appear in their headlights, only to see them disappear.

A recurring story centers around the unrest of those who died on nearby Meridean Island. These souls are said to make sounds so terrifying you can't stay in the cemetery.

Psychics and sensitives rarely enter the cemetery because of the intense feelings of unrest here.

The story of the cemetery also includes the appearance of hell hounds—but only if you turn off your headlights as you head up the hill to the cemetery. Bright idea? Sounds a little dim to me.

Spring Brook Lutheran Church

This church, also known as Caryville Church, is located relatively close to the other haunted areas of Caryville, which some claim is the most haunted spot in Wisconsin. The church and school are located on Sevestopol Road. Some say the ghost of a priest who hung himself haunts the church. This is a Lutheran church. There are no priests, so this story may not be entirely accurate.

The most widely reported story is that of a ghostly figure of a man in the bell tower, who is said to have hung himself.

If you decide to check out the church or school, you may have company. Some say that while they checked out the church, a black cat, a dog, or a trio of crows, followed them the entire time they were in the vicinity.

On an aside, I had a black dog race after my car, snarling and growling. It followed me partway to the church and schoolhouse and then disappeared. If wasn't a hellhound, but it was just as scary.

Caryville Schoolhouse

Another Caryville haunted location, another alias. This school's correct name is Spring Brook School and is located directly across from the church. This very small school (the smallest one I've ever seen) is said to be haunted by a boy who died while at school at his desk. If you sit at his desk (it's still there?!) you are said to be able to feel a rush through your body.

A boy did die while a student at the school. Seven-year-old David James Grohn died on September 24, 1957. However, he died of natural causes and did not freeze to death as has been reported.

Dark eyes have also been witnessed staring out of a rear window of the school. Other things alleged to have happened in the vicinity of the small school are the appearance of shadow demons that will pursue you once you leave the school, gusts of wind inside the building, and a familiar in the form of a black cat that just happens to have one eye and

Spring Brook Lutheran Church, Caryville.

Caryville Schoolhouse, Caryville.

three legs. This cat is said to stand guard at the entrance of the school. (I didn't see a single cat the entire time I was in Caryville.) Warning: Don't enter the school unless your familiar is bigger than the cat familiar. This means no trespassing!

City 49: Chilton

Wal-Mart

This store, located on East Chestnut Street, is not very old, yet the activities that happen in the store during the nighttime hours suggest there may be some old—and most likely restless—souls residing here.

The store is said to be built on top of an old family cemetery. The bodies were thought to have been moved before the store was built, but the guess is that some of the bodies are still there.

Items have been witnessed flying off shelves. Electrical problems, including stereos turning on or changing stations without the help of human hands, have been reported. Clean floors have been marred by muddy footprints that appear out of nowhere. Could be that little yellow roll-back guy…

City 50: Christie

Charlotte Mills Bridge

The bridge that spans the Black River in Christie is the place where a woman named Charlotte Mills took her life about a century ago. She was a mother who lived through more grief than most, and this grief most likely led to her death.

Mrs. Mills was born Charlotte A. Raymond in Manilus, New York, in 1840. Her family moved to Wisconsin when she was three. She lived near Waukesha briefly, and then moved to Fond du Lac County. She became Charlotte Ransom years later and had two sons, Fay and Benjamin. When the two boys were young, Mr. Ransom died and Charlotte remarried. Calvin John Mills, her husband, took her and her sons to Christie a few years later. They had a son, Claude Lee, together in 1877.

Charlotte's grief began in earnest in 1883 with the death of her father. In 1901, her son, Fay, drowned in Alaska. On the heels of her first son's death, was the death of her second son. Benjamin died in Idaho in 1902. As if this wasn't enough grief, her second husband died in 1905.

She somehow lived with this surfeit of grief until her advancing years. On what would be the last day of her life, she told her remaining son, Claude, that she was going to visit a friend. After she didn't return that night, Claude began searching for her. He followed her footprints, found her shawl, and finally her body floating in the river near shore.

Claude later discovered that his mother had left the house prepared; Charlotte had laid out the clothes on the bed that she wanted to be buried in.

Many farmers have seen Charlotte's ghost on or near the bridge. Others say they have seen a white "floaty" human shape near shore.

City 51: Custer

House on Long Road

Michelle Laucke, a former resident of Custer, told me this story.

"Me and my husband bought a very old farm house on Long Road. Entities there ranged from voices, to phantom kittens, to hovering forms, to nothing but our earth-based dogs growling and hackling at apparently something that we could not see. But, let's start with the move in, our first day at the old place. "Brett, my husband, was on the second floor in a closet that had slanted ceilings and old log walls and some recently added shelves. The floor looked original and was made of worn hardwood. I was in the basement made of old rocks and mortar, so we were two floors apart. I hear Brett yelling from the upstairs and went to investigate. He asked me where I had been hiding. Confused, I asked him what he was talking about. He said, 'Why did you tell me to get out?'

"Again confused, I asked him what the heck was he talking about. He said he found a loose board in the old unfinished closet and heard a deep male voice say, 'Get out!' as he tried to lift the board. He thought I was playing a trick on him.

"I asked him how could I lower my voice and talk to him when I was in the basement the whole time."

Michelle says Brett was shaken and insisted she had been playing some kind of joke on him—but she hadn't. During their stay there, their dogs would often look up the stairs leading to the second floor and hackle up and growl as if someone was up there.

"We'd go check and nothing was there, but the temperature was always cooler. This was the upstairs, and an old poorly insulated house. Trust me, it should have been warmer, not cooler.

"Then a year after we were at the house, my young sister-in-law, around age eight, slept over and used one of the upstairs rooms. She came down the next morning and asked us where the cat was, as she wanted to play with it again. We did not have a cat, nor was there one in the house. She insisted the cat was on her bed all night chasing a ball with a bell. We went to look. There was no ball, and of course no cat.

"Then a few months after my dad died, my husband and I were sleeping in the main bedroom on the main floor. It was a small room, with our king-sized canopy bed butted up against the only window in the room. It was very late at night and I awoke to what I thought was someone shining a light into our bedroom. I thought, who the heck is here and parked their car facing our bedroom window (the driveway led past our bedroom outside)? So I sat up, looked out the window, and it was pitch black. I mean black, no light was coming from outside, yet the bedroom was lit up around the bed and canopy drapes, but not like a light from the ceiling. It was a shimmer, a glow, a blurry glow all around the bed. As I started to panic, a sense of calm was voiced into my head and I started to look closely at the glowing around the bed. There were people there, numerous people, and it felt like I knew them, but I couldn't see faces, just outlined shapes, and these too were see-through. Their clothing was not discernable, but the shapes of people were. It was like a choir saying life would be okay. I still felt panicked and tried to wake Brett up. As he woke up, everything went black. The shapes and voices were gone as if nothing had been there in the first place. Brett said he didn't see anything, but thought there had been light just before he opened his eyes. "I did have another cousin say when he slept over at our house that he thought it was haunted, and he'd never stay there at night again. He would not say what he saw, heard, or felt, just that our upstairs was too creepy and he was freaked out."

City 52: Dehli

Indian Burial Grounds

Once upon a time, Dehli was a thriving town. Now it's a ghost town. Stress the word *ghost*.

This former town still has a couple of roads that didn't disappear along with the people: Dehli Road and Broadway Road. You'll find them between the towns of Omro and Eureka.

A French Canadian trader named Luke LaBorde and his Indian wife, Louisa, traveled down the Fox River and set up a trading post on Dehli's shores in 1848. LaBorde christened the area LaBorde's Landing, but later renamed it Delhi. Taking it one step further, he built a town around his trading post. Streets were laid out, including Dehli and Broadway (along with Main, Water, Menominee, and Union). Dehli enjoyed a brief boom time, but slowly declined because of its inability to compete with the wealthier bridge building towns of Omro and Eureka.

If you're wondering where this story is going, I'll tell you: to the grave. The town was literally built on a grave; more precisely, Indian burial grounds. During the first years of the town, all sorts of goodies were plowed from the earth, including bones, bones, and more bones.

Some that visit the almost non-existent town of Dehli say they feel a spiritual presence. Others say the old abandoned cemetery holds the key to who haunts the ghost town. Luke LaBorde and his wife, Louisa, are buried there. Some say they've seen ghostly figures of men dressed in old-time clothing against the horizon and that the figures disappear as you watch them.

City 53: Dewhurst

Dewhurst Lone Grave Cemetery

This gravesite, that boasts one lone gravestone, is located about thirteen miles west of Neillsville. However, it is final resting place of not one grave, but many others.

The grave of Blanche Grimes is surrounded by a white picket fence and lies near a snowmobile trail on a hill at the corner of Poertner Road and Fisher Avenue in Columbia County. A man named Knut Wiggins donated the land many years ago. Now it is a popular stopping place for the curious, who often leave flowers, stuffed animals, and coins.

Blanche Grimes was the daughter of Frank and Emma Grimes. She was born April 1, 1894 and died August 5, 1895. No one seems to be sure how she died, but it is known that Blanche's sister, Rose of Hillsboro, visited the grave twice a year for sixty years and that Blanche's aunt took care of the picket fence every year until 1969. The fence is still in good shape; it is not known who looks after the grave now.

There are believed to be twenty-seven graves here, but only one—Blanche Grimes' —is marked by a granite marker.

The people known to be buried here died in a variety of ways, some suddenly. Stories of actual ghostly figures as well as machine malfunction have been reported in the vicinity of the graves.

City 54: Eau Claire

Banbury Place

A tenant who was accidentally electrocuted here is said to make himself known on occasion. Some say they've heard—in addition to the strange sound of an old air conditioning unit—screams and painful moans, apparently the ghost reliving, or should I say re-dying, the accident that took his life.

The stories about Banbury usually center around building number 13. Shadowy figures have been seen making their way down Banbury Place's hallways. So if the tenant is haunting this area, he may have ghostly company.

This building is also said to have a maze of underground tunnels in which homeless people sometimes take refuge.

Cameron House, Eau Claire.

Cameron House

Mr. Allen Cameron, a wealthy logging baron, died in 1907 of a heat stroke in an upstairs room. His funeral was held downstairs in the parlor, where most of the ghostly activity seems to be centered.

This large house, located at 620 5th Avenue, is known for doors opening and closing on their own, flashes of light, cold spots, and items that go missing. There's even one report of empty dishes on the kitchen table exploding.

Past tenants say they've experienced episodes where their beds shook violently. Even stranger, one group of female tenants said that pizza was delivered several times to the home with one of their names on it even when she hadn't ordered it.

I spoke to a student who was friends with a former renter. She said her friend "always had a freaky story about something that broke or flew through the air or jumped off the floor."

Mr. Cameron was buried in Lakeview Cemetery in Eau Claire, but seems to still prefer his earthly home.

Fire Station No. 10

Apparently old firefighters can't be extinguished. The building is said to be haunted by a former fireman, Alex Arnie Blum, who died in 1981 of heart disease.

Firefighters have seen things ranging from pots and pans flying off the wall, apparitions of Blum, and doors—we're talking heavy doors—opening and closing on their own. What makes this haunting so unique is the fact that 80 percent of current firefighters are said to have seen Blum.

Interview with Kassandra Lee and Matt Walker

Kassandra Lee and her fiancé, Matt Walker, currently live in Eau Claire, but their interest in the paranormal sometimes takes them beyond the city limits. One example is a recent trip to nearby Caryville.

I asked Lee what made her and Walker decide to visit Caryville. "We have both heard a lot about Caryville from books and hearsay, so we thought we'd check it out. Matt's brother also had an experience at Caryville, so that was probably the main reason we chose to check it out."

This wasn't Lee's only foray into paranormal territory. She previously lived in Augusta and had been to Chainey Bridge, better known as "Green Eyes," with her fiancé, too. But it's her Caryville experience she will never forget.

Lee says the first time they visited Caryville, it was November 1, the day before her birthday and was during the daytime. The second time they were there with friends, it was at night and they visited all the spots in and around Caryville said to be haunted.

Lee says, "The night we had the experience, we hadn't seen/heard anything until Matt and a couple went to the schoolhouse." She didn't go into the schoolhouse, because when they reached Caryville, she had a strange feeling in her stomach. She says it was "a feeling that felt like we shouldn't be there, so I chose to stay in the car."

She says, "The only light source Matt and our friends had was their phones, and a lighter that our friend, Kevin, had. After entering the schoolhouse, Kevin saw an old beat up piano, so he thought he'd plunk a few notes on it."

Walker remembers what happened like it was yesterday: "We saw a shadowy figure in the corner of the room while Kevin was playing the piano. Once I pointed out the figure, Kevin then stopped playing the piano and the figure had dropped from the corner of the room down to the floor and looked as if it disappeared. Then, shortly after, Kevin's lighter seemed to have been slapped out of his hand, landing on the other side of the room. After we had left the schoolhouse was when we figured out that the shadowy figure had to have been 'Blackie.'"

It was then that the group in the building noticed a shadowy figure near where Kevin's lighter had landed. They came out of the schoolhouse and approached one of the side windows to make sense of the shadow. Except they couldn't.

They figured out that there was no way a shadow could've been cast in the room with the angle of the window and the light outside. "This was enough to scare Matt and the others away from the schoolhouse."

After leaving the schoolhouse, the group headed to the haunted boat landing. "We turned off the car as well as the lights on the car to wait for hellhounds to appear. We didn't hear anything out here, but Matt saw that same shadowy figure that they had seen in the schoolhouse, now in the rear view mirror of the car." That was enough of the boat landing.

"We then headed up to the haunted cemetery, but nothing strange happened there, so we decided to leave," says Lee. It should be noted that a couple weeks after leaving Caryville that time, Walker told Lee that he felt as if he was being followed by the shadowy figure they had seemingly picked up in Caryville.

Lee says she would definitely like to check out Caryville again, but next time she'd be more prepared with a camera and some flashlights.

And maybe some extra batteries...and a cross and some holy water?

Stone's Throw Entertainment Center

This bar slash club is located at 304 Eau Claire Street. Nearly all former and current employees say they've heard footsteps downstairs in the old kitchen hallways, or other activities like beer bottles breaking and flying across the room on their own. The ghost said to be haunting this beautiful old building is said to have committed suicide in the building, though this claim has not been substantiated.

A former waitress in her mid-twenties, who does not want to be named, said this about the bar: "There was no logic to a lot of what happened there. Things popped off shelves, and I even had a beer bottle levitate off the bar and fly straight at me." She says she wanted to quit then and there, but couldn't afford to. "I'll never forget one time," she recalls, "I was walking into the kitchen to get something, and something I couldn't see brushed past me. Except it went through me, instead of past me. I can't even begin to tell you how uncomfortable it was, mentally and physically. Needless to say, I finally quit that night."

One ghost story involves a bartender jokingly calling to everyone to get out after the bar was already clear of people. Suddenly a man got up from where he was sitting, shook out his coat and went to the door. A human would have walked through it. This man disappeared into thin air.

Stone's Throw Entertainment Center, Eau Claire.

UW—Eau Claire

Kjer Theatre is said to be haunted by Earl Kjer, the founder. He's been seen sitting in his usual seat and is said to be responsible for the odd things that happen with the curtains, lights, and props.

The theater is located on the corner of Garfield and Park Avenues and was built in 1951. Mr. Kjer died in 1965, but still hangs around to make sure things are just so in his beloved theater.

City 55: Egg Harbor

Shipwrecked Restaurant, Brewery, and Inn

Lots of ghosts are said to haunt the inn, but not simultaneously. This might be bad for ghost aficionados, but good for those with a weak heart. What's really cool about this establishment is that they even have a "Ghosts" tab on their Web site.

Shipwrecked, located in downtown Egg Harbor at 7792 Egg Harbor Road, is also famous for being Door County's only microbrew. You can enjoy six varieties of hand-crafted beer along with seasonal favorites at the full bar or outside on the patio. Just as many travel to the Shipwrecked to check out the brew house and restaurant as do to check out the ghosts.

When the inn and restaurant opened in the late 1800s, it was popular among the locals for its fine food. It was also a favorite of lumberjacks, sailors, and weary stagecoach travelers who would undoubtedly get a great meal and a great night's rest.

The 1920s may be when the people began hanging around the Shipwrecked after they died. This is the time period when Door County became a favorite "disappearing" spot for Al Capone, the famous mobster from Chicago.

Even now, there are tunnels beneath the building which are now closed for safety reasons. I learned these tunnels lead all over Egg Harbor, including Murphy Park. Capone was known to have used Murphy Park for quick getaways. Chief Tecumseh, of the Ottawa tribe, is also believed to have used these tunnels for quick getaways from other tribes.

Two revenuers, an old way of saying IRS agents, were rumored to have been last seen in this building looking for Capone. Did the two federal agents somehow get lost in the tunnels? Perhaps with a little help from Capone?

Speaking of Capone—his illegitimate son, Jason, was found dead, hanging in the attic. By his lonesome, or with a little help, is anyone's guess. Jason was believed to have been about to turn Capone (yes, his father) in to the authorities. Jason's ghost appears so lifelike that people sometimes call in to Shipwrecked when they see the boy believed to be Jason on the roof. Jason is usually spotted in the attic, but less now that it has been renovated.

Verna Moore, who was married and divorced from one of the previous owners, is the ghost most often seen at Shipwrecked. She didn't die at the inn; she passed away at her home on County EE about twenty years ago. Apparently, she then moved back to Shipwrecked. Verna's been seen walking through the dining room. She was said to be a kind woman in life, and usually appears that way in life, though one person I spoke to said the woman ghost she saw had a sour look on her face. Verna has been heard speaking in the basement, but usually makes herself known when something is about to go wrong; she's as helpful in death as she was in life.

Long ago, in the late 1800s before the Shipwrecked was in its present location, a logger was rumored to have been murdered here. His cantankerous ghost used to visit the bar. The bad boy logger hasn't been seen in a while, and no one is complaining.

Another famous ghostly duo is that of a mother and her baby. The mother was one of Capone's "girlfriends." Her baby disappeared; the next day she disappeared. Many have seen the frantic mother searching for her baby. Some say they've heard the cry of a baby when none are around.

A female traveler dressed in Victorian-era clothing, carrying a carpetbag, has also been seen inside the entrance of Shipwrecked. Would someone please tell her the stagecoach doesn't stop here anymore?

And last, but not least: Native American spirits are said to appear and disappear just that quick. Chief Tecumseh? Braves from another tribe? These Native American spirits are said to be wearing 1800s attire.

Chances are excellent you'll have something exciting to remember your trip by, and I'm not talking just great food and brew.

City 56: Elk Mound

The Overlook Tower

Located at N435 Holly Avenue, this park is said to be haunted. The Overlook Tower, a twenty-foot-high stone and mortar tower gives visitors a 360 degree view of the surrounding area. But you probably won't be able to see for yourself; the tower is no longer accessible.

Screaming, howling, and laughing can be heard when no one is there. In addition to the spooky sounds you may hear there, some have reported seeing mists and odd lights. Other says orbs turn up in photos taken there.

Stories of someone dying here, either by natural means or by falling from the tower may be just that, but most don't care. Visitors to the park say they've seen and heard enough to convince them that the tower is haunted.

City 57: Fond Du Lac

Galloway House

This stately house, completed in 1880, is located at 336 Old Pioneer Road. While you're there, take a tour of the entire historical park. Chances are good you'll either get the feeling you're not alone, or you'll hear invisible people moving around and talking in one of the mansion's thirty rooms.

This house, unlike many others that are deemed haunted, doesn't have cold spots, nor does it have anything visual to suggest it is haunted.

The reason some say it's haunted: Ghostly giggling has been heard by many in the playroom of the Galloway House. Plates have also been heard clattering in the kitchen.

Galloway House, Fond du Lac.

The former slave quarters are off limits. Some say this is the most haunted place in the house, but no one knows for sure what goes on there. Others say the place never had slaves because of Wisconsin's strong anti-slave sentiment. It is believed by many that the slave quarters were really just rooms for some of Galloway's workers.

Historic 1856 Octagon House

1856. Really? This house really doesn't look a day over 1860!

Seriously, this unique house was one part of the Underground Railroad, a hideout, actually. The ghosts said to haunt this house are slaves that are still hiding in the nine passageways and one tunnel that are part of the house.

Those that go through the house say the sound of faint crying and yelling can sometimes be heard. Even more unnerving, the sound of scratching on the wall and the sound of faint pounding can also be heard. The owners' pets, poor things, are harassed by unseen movements and noises.

A little boy ghost has been witnessed wandering through the house along with shadows that cast themselves on the walls that don't belong to anything.

Some people who tour that house occasionally succumb to bouts of nausea. And just because it's nighttime, don't think the ghosts of

Historic Octagon House, Fond du Lac.

the Octagon House rest. This is also when the living in the house see strange lights and hear odd sounds. Items move around on their own and sometimes disappear completely. One incredible thing that took place here: A spinning wheel on display was in one piece one moment, and then completely taken apart just one moment later.

While some houses increase in value because of their ghostly inhabitants, this one is said to have lost value. I don't know about you, but I think it would be fantastic to own a house with so much built-in history. It's located in a beautiful neighborhood and is really quite lovely.

Ramada Plaza

This building was formerly the Retlaw Hotel. A former owner, Walter Schroeder, was said to have been murdered on the property. He wasn't murdered at the hotel, and he didn't die there, either, but he is believed to be here now. By the way, did you notice that Retlaw is Walter spelled backwards?

Many have many seen apparitions of the former owner. Many have heard screaming and banging on walls and watched faucets and lights

81

turn on by themselves. The latter is usually not associated with the apparition of Schroeder, who was a very well-liked and respected man and philanthropist.

If you look up this hotel on the Internet and check travel sites, you will finds all sorts of former visitors who aren't shy about sharing stories about their stays at the hotel. Without fail, all agree the Ramada is charming, clean, and a great place to stay. There's another thing many agree with—the hotel is *soooooo* haunted.

One guest said while she was in the elevator on the way up to the seventh floor, a couple who was staying on the same floor told her the hotel was haunted. She didn't believe them until later that night when she heard a noise in the bathroom. She went to investigate, but found nothing amiss. However, it was at this time that she heard what sounded like footsteps in the room near her bed. She went back into the room with the bed but found nothing strange. Undoubtedly thinking it was only a dream, she went back to bed and sleep. Later, she awoke to the feeling of being held in someone's arms.

Another guest enjoyed the hotel itself, but was nonetheless disquieted by one experience there. While sleeping, the guest awoke to the feeling that an invisible someone was resting their hand on his chest. It wasn't entirely

Ramada Plaza, Fond du Lac.

unpleasant; the experience was likened to how your mother might place her hand on your chest when you're a child to calm you down. The guest said the room was secure the entire time he was at the hotel.

Other guests rave about the great food and service, but say the elevator acts up. They say this is like an invisible attendant taking over the operation of the buttons. Many guests hear footsteps in their rooms when they are alone. Another experience many guests share: Someone they can't see will sit down on their beds. Sometimes the guest is already in bed and can feel the bed shift beneath the weight of the invisible guest. Other times, the guest is not in bed, but can hear footsteps, and then will be able to watch the edge of the bed sag under the invisible weight.

The Ramada Plaza is located at 1 North Main Street.

St. Mary's Springs High School and Seminary

The story is about a nun and her baby. The nun was said to have delivered a stillborn baby in the elevator and then killed herself—with her cross. Her presence is felt along with the faint sound of a crying baby. The crying baby is still said to be heard in the seminary during the night.

The high school and seminary sit side by side on a hill at the edge of Fond du Lac at 255 County K. The seminary has a tall tower; the school has about 250 students.

City 58: Galesville

Ghost Road

How could I not include a short story about a road named "Ghost Road?"

To get there, take Highway 53 east out of Galesville. McKeeth Road, the proper name for Ghost Road, is about two miles southwest of Galesville. A man who was killed in an accident still makes himself known in ghostly form.

City 59: Glenbeulah

Glenbeulah Graveyard

This graveyard's biggest claim is the apparitions seen moving about in the graveyard during the day and even at night.

It has a lot going on—from a glowing grave, to light images that appear on some graves, to ectoplasm that shows up in many places in the graveyard. This graveyard is also known as Walnut Grove Cemetery and Glenbeulah Cemetery.

Some say they've been followed by a nonthreatening female ghost. But perhaps the most well-known and most frightening story about Glenbeulah is the one about a man who hung himself in this cemetery located at the end of Walnut Street. His body wasn't found until his head rolled down the hill. Must have been some pretty sharp rope... Unfortunately, this cool story may be just that—a story. There are no documented cases of anyone hanging themselves here.

The road leading up to the cemetery is blocked off, but you can still access it by walking up the road to the hill where the cemetery is located. The cemetery looks very old and is. Many of the stones date to the 1800s. A second cemetery that very few know about is said to be located in the woods.

Amateurs and investigators alike often come away with photos filled with orbs and unearthly shapes and colors.

City 60: Green Bay

Brewbaker's Pub

This pub is located at 209 North Washington. The attic is empty, but somebody's up there, and they're not making a secret of it. Many have heard footsteps in the attic. When you go to check, there's no one there.

Lights in the building also inexplicably go on and off.

Green Bay Area Chamber of Commerce

This building, located at 400 South Washington is so haunted that employees often share experiences with each other. Whoever is haunting the building usually makes himself or herself known by opening the door. The thing is, when you look at the door to see who came in, the door is still tightly closed. This is said to happen on Saturdays, or when there are only few people in the building.

The Chamber of Commerce offices are housed in an old railroad depot, so the ghost could be anyone.

Titletown Brewing Company

Formerly the Dousman Street Depot, this building located at 200 Dousman Street opened to the public in 1899; it and was named to the National Register of Historic Places in 1999. The two-story building opened to the public in 1899. Waiting rooms and a ticket office were located on the first floor. The upper level housed the agent's private office along with a clubroom for C&NW Railway employees. During the depot's golden age, it was a busy hub of activity. Famous visitors include Nat King Cole, Buddy Holly, and former presidents Taft, Franklin Roosevelt, and Eisenhower.

In April 1971, regularly scheduled passenger service via the C&NW came to an end, but the depot remained a center of C&NW activity. Then, in August 1994, the building was vacated. It sat idle until 1996 when a group of investors renovated and opened the Titletown Brewing Company.

The Titletown Brewing Company is proud of the rich history of the building, and rightly so. The menu and drink selection are outstanding. While you're there, check out "The Receiver," the twenty-two-foot Packer statue that was formerly located near Lambeau Field.

As for ghosts...people have seen apparitions of people dressed in 1920s clothing as well as a train conductor wearing an old-style uniform.

Things move around by themselves in the kitchen. Spatulas and other utensils that aren't nailed down sometimes move to other locations. Kegs of beer also seem to move around on their own.

And lastly, many have reported hearing the ghostly wail of a train whistle when no trains have been here for years.

City 61: Green Lake

Dartford Cemetery

You better believe this cemetery was on my wish list of haunted Wisconsin locations! I've wanted to visit the cemetery since the very first time I heard about it.

Located in town on North Street, it is said to be haunted by an Indian chief who once lived and ruled in the Green Lake area, Civil War soldiers, and an entire family, whose children were believed to have died of polio. The mausoleum that holds the graves for the family is said to be the most haunted spot in the cemetery. If you sit on the roof of the crypt you can see from the entrance of the cemetery, you will get pushed off. With all this activity, you have to wonder how anyone can rest in peace here.

If you come to this cemetery, you shouldn't be surprised to see shadows or apparitions. Many do, but mostly on the older half of the cemetery which is separated by a city street. You also shouldn't be surprised to hear ghostly noises. Feel like you're being followed around? You probably are. Many feel ghostly presences day and night. Orbs are regularly captured here, too.

Dartford Cemetery, Green Lake.

The Internet is filled with experiences of those who have visited the cemetery. Some are young, some are grandparents, some walk in as believers, and some are skeptics. The interesting thing: Many leave the cemetery truly frightened.

Some recent experiences include a group of friends who went to the cemetery to see if the mausoleum story was true. The group sat on top of the crypt for about five minutes until two of the group wanted to leave. They jumped down. The other friend decided to leave, too. As she was about to get down, she was pushed. At first she thought her friends were responsible, but they were ahead of her. Truly frightened, they all raced for the car. As they looked back, two little children were running behind them. But when they got to the gate, the children were gone. As they left the cemetery, they looked in the rear view mirror and saw a woman standing at the gate with the children. One member of the group said it was the scariest moment of her life. Others have had the same thing happen, except it was in a different part of the cemetery and it was the Indian chief instead of the woman and the two children.

Some believe that spirits do exist and you can't make friends with them. They believe spirits are angry because they are trapped in an unknown place that is not their home. They may be territorial and

"Pushy" crypt in the cemetery.

sometimes do things to make trespassers go away. One woman said after sitting on a grave and smoking a cigarette, it kept extinguishing on its own. She believes the dead want their habitat to be a quiet place.

While I was there, I kept hearing the sound of "baseballs" being dropped on the ground alongside me as I walked, but I never saw anything. There are trees alongside the back of the old half of the cemetery. Either the squirrels were clumsy that day, or...

City 62: Hilbert

Hilbert Road

Urban legend? Legend based on truth? Both? Neither?

Hilbert Road, on the east side of Hilbert and also east of Lake Winnebago, is said to be haunted by a ghost. The ghostly man is said to walk the road between midnight and five o'clock in the morning. Sometimes he's carrying a lantern as he searches for his daughter who was killed on Hilbert Road long, long ago.

Some say half his face is missing—you'll notice this fact as you stop to see if he needs help.

This story sometimes features a different ghost. Some see a young girl in a white gown instead of the man. She has her entire face.

City 63: Holmen

Halfway Creek Lutheran Cemetery

Apparitions and unexplained lights have all been witnessed at the cemetery at Halfway Creek Lutheran, east of Holmen on Highway W, and the area around the Shefelbine Orchard area on Shefelbine Road, just off Highway M.

This area, between Holmen and West Salem, has been the site of human-sized mists and strange colored balls of light. Orbs often show up in photos taken at the cemetery.

Some have felt cool drafts at the cemetery. Coulee ghosts keeping their cool?

City 64: Independence

Lavender Lilly

This ghost story gets high marks (from me anyway) for the very unique name of the subject. Lavender Lilly, also spelled Lavender Lily—kinda sounds like a doll from your grandmother's china doll collection, doesn't it?

A girl named Lavender was said to have been walking home from school when she was struck by a car and killed. It's not clear what road she was actually on when she met her demise, but she's said to haunt Theisen Ridge Road. In another story, she was killed on her prom night.

Lilly, walking this road, can be seen from the cemetery where she is said to be buried.

It should be noted that Theisen Ridge Road is quite far outside the town of Independence off County X, and is located in Buffalo County, not Trempeleau County. The cemetery Lavender Lilly would most likely be buried in is the Upper Montana Ridge/St. Boniface Catholic Cemetery at County X at Coon Valley Road. The second most likely resting place would be the Lower Montana Ridge Cemetery.

I talked to people who had heard the story; but none have seen Lavender Lilly. Yet.

City 65: Institute

Institute Saloon

This saloon is located at 45999 State Highway 57 in Institute, though the mailing address is Sturgeon Bay. The bar stands on a pie-shaped piece of land in the heart of Institute, which is eight miles north of Sturgeon Bay.

Institute Saloon was built in 1897 by John Wester Sr., and served as a post office until free rural delivery was begun.

The ghost of a former owner named Mable is said to haunt the premises.

Mable is said to be responsible for opening and closing the women's restroom stall doors and flushing the toilets. Hey, ghosts like a clean bathroom, too.

Patrons have heard voices emanating from behind the bar, and sometimes accompanying shadows.

When Mable was alive she liked vodka; now empty bottles are sometimes found inside toilet tanks. Weird? Not really. This was one of Mable's favorite hiding places.

City 66: La Crosse

Barlow's Ghost

This is one ghost story that is equal parts *boo* and *boo-hoo*. It starts in 1848. A man named John Barlow came to La Crosse; disease took his wife and child from him and he became a recluse.

Then, out of the blue, a messenger came to tell Barlow he had inherited a fortune from his family in England. His good fortune only lasted a few days, however. When his neighbors went to his "hut" at the intersection of West and Cameron Avenues, John Barlow and the hapless messenger were found murdered. The murder was never solved.

The owners of Barlow's property didn't stay long after purchasing it. Eight months was all it took for the phantom to drive them away. This same phantom also made itself known to passersby. The apparition would walk along Cameron and West Avenues, making "queer and mysterious noises" before disappearing.

The haunting continued until 1905, when the cornerstone of the First Evangelical Lutheran Church was laid, you guessed it, at Cameron and West Avenues.

Bodega Brew Pub

This pub is located at 120 South 4th Street was at one time called the Union Saloon. The ghost said to haunt the premises belongs to a former pool hall owner, Paul Malin. When he owned the business in the late 1800s, it was called the Malin Pool and Sample Room. After he died in 1901, the building changed hands a number of times. A.J. Hines, another owner didn't keep the property for very long. He told

Bodega Brew Pub, La Crosse.

friends he was selling because he'd had it with the ghost of Malin, whom he believed was not only making noises, but was out of control.

The Bodega Brew Pub is a popular bar located on a high-traffic street which serves 400 different types of beers. That's a lot, even for Wisconsin.

It's not known whether Malin is still hanging here. If he is, he probably has a hard time making his presence known. The place is packed almost every night.

Del's Bar

If you're gonna have a ghost-in-residence, it's nice to have a helpful ghost. La Crosse's legal crowd has been stopping by this popular watering hole for almost eighty years. The oval bar inside the bar, by the way, is an icon in itself. It serves as an informal roundtable for topics ranging from local and national politics to the Green Bay Packers. The biggest ghost story associated with Del's has to do with the manager, who happened to be sitting behind the bar in a chair before opening one day.

He heard knocking at the door, went to answer it, but got a big surprise before he got there. A large iron ceiling fan that had been directly above the chair he had been sitting in, fell onto the chair crushing it.

The manager didn't find anyone at the door and no one was near the bar, as the bar was empty except for him—and the helpful ghost that prevented great bodily harm or death. No one is sure who is haunting the bar; guesses range from a former owner to patron to someone who lived down the street.

Whether you come in to Del's to discuss politics or possible ghostly experiences in the mucho neon-lit bar, you won't be bored. Del's is located at 229 3rd Street North.

Hydrite Chemical Company

The building where terror and death occurred has been razed along ago. That said, some say they still feel something "bad" in this area.

The old Hydrite Chemical Company was the site of some of the worst industrial poltergeist activity ever recorded. The worst of it took place near the turn of the nineteenth century, and is attributed to an employee who committed suicide there in the 1890s. This nasty ghost was seen by employees, managers, and watchmen, and struck fear into any who were privy to it.

Employees at the old chemical company knew they were in for some really bad business if they heard the sound of the wind picking up in the distance. As it grew in power, the sound would border on deafening, then stop completely. This was when the terror began.

Witnesses would then hear a crazed laugh, followed by objects being launched through the air with ghostly fury. If you hung around, you'd then hear the presence make its way through the wall to an abandoned area above the offices where the previously mentioned employee was said to have committed suicide.

The poltergeist wasn't seen just by Hydrite employees; three different companies that had operations in the building also experienced poltergeist activity.

Some say the poltergeist had something to do with the death of plant owner, George Pierce, who died in 1903 in his office. He had been sleeping overnight at his desk. The majority of ghostly activity ceased once the old building was razed and a new one was built. However, some say the spirit still lingers in the form of a "really creepy feeling that makes the hair on the back of your neck stand up, like someone's about to do something bad to you."

Hydrite Chemical Company is located at 701 Sumner Street.

Old Holmbo House

This is a private residence that never seems to escape mention as being haunted when talking about the La Crosse area. The owner of the house, Nicolai Holmbo, exited life in a very sad way; he hung himself in the front room of the house located at 1419 Logan Street on August 1, 1904.

His earthly body was buried, but his spirit stayed put in the house. Mr. Holmbo apparently didn't know he was dead, because neighbors regularly heard sad cries and often saw white apparitions inside the deserted house.

Lights were reported on inside the house, though no one was inside to turn them on. Even worse, some saw the ghost frantically waving his arms about. The police were summoned to the empty house, but found no one there.

The address of the house, which was still standing in 2002, was changed to 1319 Logan Street.

City 67: Manitowoc

Evergreen Inn Hotel

The words *death* and *suicide* are associated with this former hotel, and so is the word *ghosts*. Many are believed to have ended their lives here. One room in particular is said to be haunted by a woman who killed herself at this location.

At other times, the lounge of this tall building in downtown Manitowoc was also the setting for ghostly activity, but of a more festive variety. Ghostly people wearing 1900s clothing have been seen dancing and eating here.

The elevator is not exempt from ghostly activity, either. Sometimes the elevator will stop at floors that are not on the route. Some say ghostly visitors are being picked up and dropped off.

Another story associated with the former hotel is that of the sound of someone pounding on the floor above a restaurant in the building. Four people from the restaurant went to investigate, found nothing, but heard more noise on the stairs. According to the story, police and a K-9 unit went through, but found nothing.

The Evergreen Inn Hotel is now an apartment building known as the Manitowoc Place Apartments and is located at 204 North 8th Street.

St. Mary's Nursing Home

This complex of buildings, located at 2005 Division Street, was an orphanage in the early 1900s. To this day, children and a dog have been witnessed running through the towers and playing. Along with the children, a man was been seen walking his dog down the hallways. If you ask him what he's doing there, he vanishes. I'm guessing his dog does, too.

Many of the nursing home's current residents comment on, or complain about, noisy children and a barking dog.

Nurses that work there say doors slam for no reason and call lights mysteriously turn on. Though the upstairs is said to be the most haunted area, those who work there say the basement is just as haunted. Nuns used to live there and a white ghostly figure has been seen making its way down the hallways.

Whether you are alone or with others, you often get the feeling that you are being pushed. Inexplicable cold spots are prevalent throughout the basement which consists of many closed-off areas.

A nurse who worked at Centers 2 and 3 witnessed many odd occurrences. The one that sticks out in her mind is that of a see-through woman who sits by the corridor window.

This nurse also said residents complain about a child jumping on their beds when no children are there. While the nurse hasn't seen or heard any ghostly children, she's seen an adult ghost in the hallways in Center 3.

St. Mary's was once operated by the Felician Sisters. That might explain why staff and residents have seen nuns in habits in the basement.

City 68: Marshfield

Haunted Apartment

Sheri Reading and her fiancée, Dustin Dekarske, live in Marshfield. Reading says their current Marshfield address is not haunted. However, their former apartment, located at S2778 State Highway 13, Marshfield, was haunted. Reading not has not only witnessed a number of different eerie occurrences; she believes she knows who is responsible.

The ghost? Reading isn't sure what his real name was in life, but she's named him "Tom." The bedroom of the apartment she and Dekarske shared is where Tom was shot, abruptly ending his earthly life. To this day, it is not known whether Tom shot himself, or the other person there with him did the deed. Oddly, and perhaps luckily, nothing unearthly ever happened in the bedroom where Tom passed away, but Tom did make his presence known elsewhere in the apartment.

When Dekarske's daughter, Fallyn, was asleep in her crib, Dekarske would sometimes go to the back hallway, just outside their apartment, to have a cigarette. On more than one occasion he would hear a bag of cans rustle—loudly—from inside the apartment. No one but his daughter was in the apartment. Alarmed, he would go back inside the apartment to see who or what was making the noise, only to find his daughter awake, cooing, and cawing in her crib. Not only that, she'd be waving her hands and laughing as if communicating with someone—only it was a someone Dekarske couldn't see.

Was Tom rustling the cans to get Dekarske's attention so he would know Fallyn was awake? Apparently, Tom had a way with babies; Fallyn was always happy and content after these can-rustling episodes.

Tom made himself know in another way: Sometimes when Dekarske was asleep, he'd awake to the sound of "white noise" over the baby monitor. Tom again—telling Dekarske he should check on Fallyn? Makes sense to me.

Reading said they also had a pendulum clock when they lived at the apartment. It worked fine for a while, then the pendulum got a mind of its own. Swing. Not swing. Swing… A malfunction, or Tom just having a little fun?

Reading says they moved this past winter to their current address. She says she remembers packing the clock and the pendulum before the move, but when they unpacked at their new place, the pendulum was gone.

Makes one wonder if Tom wanted a keepsake to remember their stay with him…

Old County Hospital

The reason this old barn-like building, more commonly called "Old Norwood," is considered haunted is because a number of patients have either died or committed suicide here. An underground tunnel is said to link the building to a building on other side of the road. This tunnel is also said to be haunted.

This is first place in Marshfield that people name when asked if there are any haunted places. I remember hearing about Old Norwood thirty years ago. High school kids from schools more than an hour away would come here to see the ghostly figures and lights in the building, and hear the ghostly screaming in the abandoned building.

The building, located on Galvin Avenue, is on the outskirts of town in a business park. You can still see the words "Wood County Hospital Farm" on the outside of the structure.

Old County Hospital, Marshfield.

St. Joseph's Hospital

Nurses in the newest part of the hospital say the older nurses in the old part of the building still talk about ghosts passing through places that have been torn down and rebuilt.

St. Joseph's Hospital, Marshfield.

In the old mental health area of the hospital, ghosts were seen by many in the mid-1900s. The ghosts were said to be "young" and always wore a hospital gown. They never talked to anyone, but wandered aimlessly down the hallways, turning their head this way and that and then disappearing into thin air.

Another ghost that has been mentioned repeatedly is one that walks around 4 West wearing a black robe. Hopefully, this is a "regular" ghost and not the Grim Reaper variety.

The hospital, founded more than 100 years ago by the Sisters of the Sorrowful Mother, is located at 611 St. Joseph Avenue.

City 69: Menasha

Menasha High School

What a beautiful high school, haunted or not. The tunnels, said to still exist beneath this red brick building in the 1940s, are believed to be haunted. The tunnels once connected Menasha High

Menasha High School, Menasha.

with Butte des Morts School in case of a nuclear attack. The reason for the ghosts—four students got caught in the tunnel while playing hooky and died.

These hapless student ghosts are said to still be trying to get out by pounding and screaming. The school for grades 9-12 is located at 420 7th Street.

Valley Road

Some have seen a dead groom hanging from a tree by his bowtie alongside this road. He was the victim of a gruesome accident that took place more than a hundred years ago.

The poor man, on his way to what should have been the happiest day of his life, somehow tangled with a tree on the side of the road. His bowtie strangled him to death.

On certain nights—I'm guessing the anniversary of the gruesome event—you are able to see the groom hanging there. Valley Road is a very long road; good luck finding the location. No one I spoke to knew the exact spot, though some believe it's near a big curve in the road.

Wiowash Trail

This trail starts at Carl Steiger Park in Oshkosh, but it's the part of the trail in Menasha that has yielded some paranormal events that are not usually part of a well-used trail.

First of all, you might ask: What is Wiowash? You might guess a Native American tribal leader or a new self-cleaning car. It's actually an acronym composed of letters of the counties the trail passes through: Winnebago, Outagamie, Waupaca, and Shawano.

The Wiowash trail is open the entire year and is used by pedestrians, bicyclists, hikers, joggers, and even horseback riders, cross country skiers, and snowmobilers.

It is also said to get some use from things that aren't exactly human. Ghosts and demons are also said to use the trail on occasion. Some who have used the park at night have been "attacked" and "chased" by spirits with red eyes. These beings also growl. But don't get too freaked out: These paranormal occurrences did not happen along the entire trail, only one section of the trail in Menasha. One student at UW-Oshkosh said she heard growling and could see something ghostly running behind her bicycle at dusk. The animal-type apparition disappeared when she met a group of people walking.

Another person said they had an experience near the cemetery. This stretch of the trail is believed to have been an Indian burial ground that was dug up for a railroad that led to a factory nearby. The area is now residential, and the warehouse is now an apartment building.

Marty, a Milwaukee-based paranormal investigator, has also had experiences on the trail that happened between 9 and 11 pm, during an informal walk hosted by a local group. "I came up to walk with the group and do some investigations of my own," he says. "I should mention I'm a sensitive as well (I grew up around mediums and the Morris Pratt society), so my ability to track and interact with entities and/or paranormal phenomena is of course greater than the bulk of the people on those walks. On the few times I came there, there were other sensitives as well, who were also able to pick up and/or confirm some of the detected phenomena."

The two times Marty was at Menasha, he was choked and had to catch his breath. He came away with an incredible EVP from during the initial attack as well as intriguing photos.

This wasn't the first time he's been attacked—and it won't be the last. Like other investigators, he's been choked, scratched, made extremely nauseous, etc. Marty says it comes with the territory of putting yourself specifically in areas where you're called on to directly interact (i.e. investigating) entities that may or may not have good intent.

Marty is dedicated. He says that no matter what happens, it doesn't make him want to give up, though—just learn how to better protect himself. "If anything, it gives me more of a desire to deal with the situation so other people are safe."

All I can say is thank goodness for people like Marty who help those of us who are striving to find answers to our paranormal questions, or at least a better understanding.

City 70: Menomonie

Caddie Woodlawn Park

Caddie Woodlawn, a book character, was born Caroline Augusta Woodhouse, and lived on this site when she was growing up. Woodhouse's granddaughter, Carol Ryrie Brink, detailed her grandmother's adventures with her red-headed brothers in her award-winning books.

Caddie's sister, Mary, one of the eight children in the family, is buried in an unmarked grave on the property. It is the ghost of Mary that is believed to be the shadowy figure that will follow you at the park. In addition, cold spots are felt throughout the park, and footsteps have been heard on the second floor of the cabin, despite the fact that no one earthly is there.

Devil's Punch Bowl Scientific Study Area

Devil's Punch Bowl is located on 410th Street outside of Menomonie. Some say the circle of bedrock not only looks haunted, it is. No word on why or by whom.

Other visitors see strange balls of light, white ghostly shapes, and gnome-like figures. Yes, gnomes.

Some say if they take water from the park, the temperature never changes. Don't go here after dark. Not only is it illegal, it's just plain not safe.

Mabel Tainter Theater

This theater is located at 205 Main Street E. The ghost or ghosts said to haunt this incredible building could be any of a number of women or men. It's anyone's guess, because no one is known to have died on the premises.

The theater is not far from the University of Wisconsin-Stout and is named for Mabel Tainter, who passed away at the young age of nineteen. Captain Andrew and Bertha Tainter spared no expense in constructing the incredible building as a tribute to their daughter.

Architect Harvey Ellis was commissioned to build the two- to three-story building made out of Dunville sandstone. It's predominantly crafted in the Richardsonian Romanesque style, but also has Moorish touches. This theater has 313 seats, a marble staircase and floors, leaded windows, and oak and walnut woodwork. It's beautiful!

The female ghost seen in the theater is believed to be Mabel Tainter, even though she died four years before it was built. Many believe it is her mother, Bertha, making sure things are running smoothly. Others think it may be a departed stage hand. Still others think it may be a coed from the nearby university who died at a young age. And some think the ghost is a young Unitarian woman or patron; the theater is home to The Unitarian Society of Menomonie. Whew! It really *could* be anyone!

A strange light has been witnessed in the storage area and the library, but if you go to check it out, the strange light disappears. Actors and actresses sometimes find themselves staring at an apparition who just happens to be staring at them. The sound equipment sometimes falls victim to a little paranormal tinkering, and apparitions and cold drafts are often felt in the library/reading room.

Regular people like you and me often get the feeling they are being watched. Some even report hearing a faint whispering in their ear that disappears when they turn around.

Staff are not blind to the woman ghost, either. Bathroom attendants in the women's bathroom have seen a young woman in ghostly form walk in and out of the downstairs restroom. The same young female ghostly woman has been seen looking at herself curiously in the mirror.

Another strange phenomenon is the odd ball of light that has been witnessed in a storage room. Finally, a male staff member had a female dressed in white float past him while he was on the second floor. She didn't acknowledge him or anything else; she just went floating past.

UW-Stout

A student was rumored to have killed himself in his room at the JTC Residence Halls. The living students in this very long, three-story dorm, now sometimes hear the sound of voices in empty rooms and find doors that lock and unlock themselves.

The cafeteria is also said to be affected. Items and equipment are misplaced, and sometimes things tip over on their own.

I spoke to one former dorm resident who said he often awoke at 3 am to feel his bed being shaken violently. He swears he was not drinking, and said his room had a "creepy" feel to it whether he was the only one there, or if others were there.

The building is located at 220 South Broadway Street.

City 21: Meridean

Caryville Road

Caryville Road is really 240th Avenue, but the bridge on this infamous road, the Prom Queen Bridge, is what makes this story so haunting. One of the most unique stories about this road is what may happen to you if you look into the water as you drive over the bridge at night. You may see the phantom headlights of one of many vehicles said to have driven off the bridge into the water. The bridge is less than two miles away from County Road H.

In the first story, a beautiful girl named Jenny, on prom night, drove her pickup off the bridge after a hard night of partying. In the second story, a different girl, no name given, drove her car off the bridge when it inexplicably swerved. Her body was supposedly swept away and was never recovered.

On this road you may see headlights behind or ahead of you that suddenly disappear. You may experience a chilling of the interior of your vehicle no matter how warm it is outside.

Other stories about a woman ghost who committed suicide at the site of the bridge are sometimes mentioned. Ferry disappearances have also been mentioned near here.

Today, it's a boating and swimming area. Given its history, I don't think I'll be doing either here.

City 72: Nekoosa

Alexander Middle School

Long ago, this huge building was the high school—way before I can remember. Now it's no longer a public school of any kind. When I went to school here, it was the middle school. It wasn't haunted then, though I distinctly remember feeling very uneasy the few odd times I was alone in the hallway near the cafeteria.

For a long period of time, it was for sale and unoccupied. Now it's home to at least one business: Nekoosa Karate & Fitness occupies one part of the building.

Residents of Nekoosa, as well as passersby, have seen an old janitor ghost by himself and sometimes with a young girl at his side. He's said to haunt the third floor. I don't know of any janitors dying at school, so

Old Alexander Middle School, Nekoosa.

my guess is that it's one of the nice janitors from the past still hanging around to help any ghostly schoolchildren that might need help.

The smell of cigar smoke can still be smelt throughout the building.

Hammers and other tools were said to move on their own during construction after the school was closed.

Perhaps the biggest indicator of paranormal activity is the lights that shine in the middle of the night in third story windows. Sometimes these lights are accompanied by ghostly mists.

Greenwood Cemetery

I've been here twice; once when I was a teen, and again just recently. I've heard dozens of stories from those who've had frightening experiences here.

The area where the cemetery is located is technically the township of Armenia, in Juneau County, not Wood. The cemetery can be accessed by taking AA south out of Nekoosa until you see Plank Hill Road. It will turn into 26th Avenue North. You can't miss the cemetery on your left, though it is easy to miss 26th Avenue North.

Greenwood Cemetery, Nekoosa.

This cemetery is on a dead-end road. One side rests on the edge of a drop-off close to the river. Interestingly—or not—the word cemetery on a chest high sign is spelled "cemetary" (while cemetery is spelled correctly on the big sign over the gate).

The reason so many people go to this cemetery is the fact that a demon was seen here decades ago. In addition, ghostly beasts have also been seen here at night. And did I mention vapors that rise from graves have also been witnessed?

The area is very secluded. For your safety, don't go alone and observe all the cemetery's rules.

House on Wagonwheel Drive

This truly scary story comes from Karla Houghton, and she lets you know right away that she doesn't really believe in ghosts. But she does know she didn't imagine what happened to her—and it's something she never wants to experience again. Ever.

Houghton and her husband, Mark, rented the small ranch house on Wagonwheel Drive, in the town of Saratoga, from her sister. Houghton's sister mentioned orbs in the hallway, but Houghton says she didn't think anything of it.

Houghton lived in the house for a while when the incident occurred. She was working at a local paper mill at the time and decided to take a nap before work (the graveyard shift). Her husband joined her; he immediately fell asleep.

Houghton still gets shaky when she recalls that night. "I was trying to sleep, but couldn't. Mark was sleeping, snoring actually, and I was wishing I could sleep because I had a long night in front of me. I was on my back, looking up at the ceiling, but was suddenly aware I wasn't alone."

She says she looked down and straight in front of her, and was shocked to see a man standing at the foot of the bed. But he wasn't quite a man—he was kind of see-through. "He had dark hair and a dark beard. He was bare-chested. I don't know if he was wearing pants, because that's as much as I could see."

Her first instinct was to scream, but she couldn't. Before she could inhale, the man was straddling her torso. "I felt the bed move on each side of me and felt a crushing pressure on my chest. Suddenly he started choking me. I couldn't turn my head to look at Mark, but I could see out of the corner of my eye that he was sleeping. The man continued choking me. I couldn't breathe. The only thing I could think was that he was going to kill me if I didn't do something." It was obvious her husband was asleep and couldn't help her.

Though she's not particularly religious, she says she started praying. "I started saying Hail Marys. I don't know how many I said, or when the man disappeared, but suddenly he was gone."

The event really shook her up. So much that she was even afraid to sleep in the house after that for a while. When it came time to move out of the house, she told her sister, "You know, your house is haunted" and then told her the story about the man with the dark hair and beard that had tried to choke her.

Houghton says her sister looked stunned. She'd seen him too. Who was this man? Both sisters were raised in the area and no one remembers anyone dying in or near the house.

Wakely House

This very historic site is said to be teeming with Point Basse pioneers—if you believe the stories of those that have visited the site south of Nekoosa, just off County Z on Wakely Road. The building was constructed in 1831, and served as part of a tavern for early settlers and loggers; it was the first white settler's house in what is now Wood County. The Wakely house, now part of the Point Basse Historic Village, is adjacent to the Wisconsin River.

Restored Wakely House, Nekoosa.

The two-story restored house and cabin are places where people have spotted ghosts walking in and out. Mrs. Wakely is the person most often mentioned in association with the word "ghost."

One visitor to the site, a sensitive, says the area near the river itself "is very oppressive. I feel that a number of people, including lumbermen, died in this particular spot."

In the 1840s, the steamboats *Maid of Iowa* and *Enterprise* operated on the Wisconsin River. They carried passengers and cargo between Prairie du Chien and Point Basse. A cable ferry also operated at the Wakely site until 1916.

Among the ghosts that have been seen near the river, cabin, and house are Indians, women in long dresses, and men in "puffy shirts."

City 73: New Lisbon

Panther and Gee's Slough Effigy Mounds

Panther Effigy Mounds lies south of New Lisbon on Highways 12 and 16. It contains an ancient Native American burial ground and effigy mounds that are said to "vibrate with spiritual energy."

Gee's Slough Effigy Mounds are located in Indian Mounds Park, to the south of New Lisbon. This is the site of several effigy mounds including a rare flex-legged running panther. A linear mound and several round mounds located there were said to have been used by important members of the tribe. These Native American burial grounds are said to be filled with the spirits of the Woodland Culture people, ancestors of the Ho-Chunk, who lived in the area from 499 BC to around 1500 AD.

Visitors have reported seeing faint apparitions of Native Americans of long ago. Some are alone; sometimes sightings include groups of three to six. Many others have reported feeling chills, even when standing in strong sunlight.

Caves in this area are said to be haunted. Corroboration is difficult; most of the caves in the area are privately owned.

City 74: New London

Eagles Nest

The haunting story below, about Captain Enos Drummond, titled "The Tales of Captain Drummond," was sent to me by Angie Seidl, Director of the New London Public Museum. It was written by museum volunteer, Jim Villiesse, from research compiled by museum staff. Thank you, New London Public Museum!

The museum also holds historic homes/downtown/cemetery walks. For more information, see New London Public Museum's listing in the Attractions section of this book.

As an aside, Fred Bernegger, whom you'll read about in the story below, is one of the two founders who started Wisconsin's own Hillshire Farms.

The Tales of Captain Drummond

A vast yee land lubbers and hear the tale of the times of yore when the trade winds blew and this town was connected to the sea. I be Captain Enos Drummond, Master of many a craft which plied Lake Michigan and the inlets to Chicago thence our Fox, Winnebago, and Wolf.

I was the first master of the Schooner William Jones, the largest lumber carrying cargo vessel on any of the Great Lakes. We would sail with our timber, hewn from these north woods to the markets in Chicago bringing back new settlers and goods.

These were the times when men lived and died by the winds. There were few roads, the railroads were just skirting Wisconsin and the lakes and rivers were the main street of commerce.

The rivers were higher and wilder then. More treacherous too, filled with river pirates and bursting with logs being floated down stream.

I was honored by the City of Chicago for braving gale and storm to save my fellow sailors from Davy Jones' grip.

Twas the brigantine *Merchant* floundering in a storm, her decks already awash with the crew holding onto the mast as the storm gales struck and plunged the ill-fated crew one by one into the drink.

The *William Jones* had safely made port and the watch reported the disaster. I took a lifeboat and three of my crew and brought back five alive; there were only three lost that night. Chicago presented us all with gold watches engraved with a shipwreck for our deeds that day.

Later, in May of 1854 me thinks, another gale swept down upon us. Again safely in port was the *William Jones* but the Schooners *Maine*, *Throop* & *Hayden* were not so lucky.

I commandeered a lifeboat from the *Globe* and four volunteers to go out with me. Another lifeboat from the *Illinois* had already set out, but was forced to turn back. We passed it the storm, grim determination on our faces. The crew of the *Maine* was washing ashore alive but the worse for it. However, the *Throop* and the *Hayden* lay further out. We snatched fifteen men from the lake during that squall; only one perished from the *Hayden*. The papers made much of our efforts, but any seaman would have done the same.

But being a restless soul, I had enough of the big Lake and the long sails around the Door and down the Fox, so in 1855, I purchased a little side-wheeler steamer named *Eureka* but everybody called it the *Pickerel* as over each paddle wheel box, a big lunging pickerel was painted. I made weekly trips from Oshkosh to New London. Often up to Shawano when the river was high.

By 1858, I had a newer and better boat—the *Wolf*—and my life was at its peak.

My Hester and I had five children: Elsie, Charles, Phedora, Frank and Lilly. I had bought land back in '49 on Ledge Road in Hortonia. I began construction of a twenty-seven-room home I was gonna call the Eagles Nest. Top o'dat, I had two servants, a young girl Albena and an old negro Isaac. I even owned part of a stage line that took folks from here to Stevens Point.

Then came the day of my doom. It was the very next year. The river was high and my passengers urgently wanting to get to port. The loggers had a jam and the *Wolf* was heavily buffeted by rolling timber. I was so corn-founded mad I swore to kill the next lumberjack I saw.

Then this dang fool, Luther Martin, announces that he was a lumber baron and I should be grateful for his trade. We got to shouting and pushing, and finally, I couldn't take his insults no more, so I stabbed him with my whittling knife.

He didn't die or nothin' and the magistrate saw it my way and said self-defense. But he cursed me and like a whirlpool, everything I held dear was took.

First thing was Hester, up and died. Then my son Charles, age twelve, was my cabin boy. He fell over board and drowned in '63. That same year the *Wolf* caught fire and was lost.

By January I was dead. My house passed to my second wife, Martha, and the curse continued.

My house looked like a Southern Plantation. Martha sold it to some fool named Fenow; he had a brother who bought horses for the Union army. Seems his brother wasn't good at poker and lost all the Army's money and fled up here to hide out. Well they found him, had a big shoot out with a force sent to capture him. They won and marched him back south. Hung him I recon, don't know. Fenow fled as well. The Eagles Nest stood empty and the curse continued.

Pretty soon I wasn't remembered as a hero for saving my fellow sailors or as a river pioneer for opening up the *Wolf* clear to Shawano. No, they remembered me knifing Luther and they remembered my negro servant and soon I was a ferocious river pirate and southern sympathizer. The Eagles Nest was to be a northern plantation and it was said I already had forty slaves secreted away on the day I died.

They claimed I thought the South would win and I would control the slave market along the river.

Next thing you know my house was haunted. They claimed an army deserter had a shoot out and died there. They claimed at midnight they would hear Luther and me in a brawl at three each morning and the thud of a knife in his chest would end the fight. They claimed if you listened you could hear the chants of the Negros chained in my cellar, moaning to be set free. They even composed a poem:

> "When the calm of night has descended,
> Upon this ghostly place,
> And the shrieking, reeking sounds of the heart,
> Fill this mighty place,
> And seem to rent this structure,
> From its very foundation,
> And even at this time, set not a limitation
> As to how the chills run up and down your spine!
> Hear the light trill laughs,
> See the clammy figures stand in line,
> Their haunting hearts rending frolics,
> Heard through the long dark, chilling hours
> Till at the first peek of Dawn,
> Mysteriously gone,
> Only to return punctually at dusk.
> As you'll soon learn. If you dare this night."

Kind of spooky, eh? Seems like sensationalism isn't a new idear.

The last barnacle hit the main sail in 1965. The Eagles Nest had a new owner, Fred Bernegger, who planned on revamping the old place and was half way through this deed when, over his objections, the *Post Crescent* printed a pre-Halloween article lauding the site as Ghost Manor saying I had been murdered here by the ghost of Luther Martin to the joyous chanting of my forty slaves.

The crowd descends on all Hallowed's Eve; thousands of thrill seekers trampled the hills looking for signs of Luther, the slaves, and me... Finding nothing someone set the place on fire and by all Soul's Day it was gone and with it any memory of me.

So there you have it my lads and ladies, my tale of triumph and woe. From a time when there were just footpaths and wheel ruts and the river was the true highway and the riverboat reigned supreme.

Kind of spooky? No. *Very* spooky. You can visit the museum at 406 South Pearl Street in historic New London.

Haunted House on County T

One resident of this home on County Road T says it's haunted to the max. The young woman says her parents refuse to admit their old two-story house is haunted, even though they've also had many inexplicable experiences.

"Sarah" advises that she's known for as long as she can remember that ghosts reside with her family in the home. These ghosts talked to her when she was as young as four years old and have talked to her ever since. Sometimes, when she is tired of "listening" to them talk and tries to shut them out, they will walk through her. She says it feels like nothing you can imagine, like something is stretching through her.

While she's been living at the house, she's seen a young girl and a woman. Sarah believes they were the original owners. Others, including her parents, have also seen different ghostly people in the house.

Another house on County T is used as a haunted house during Halloween. With so many haunted houses on this road, it might be a good idea to change the name of the road to County GHOST instead of County T.

Washington High School

No one is sure if one or two ghosts haunt the school. The band room is the site of strange experiences caused by things not human. A ghost is believed to communicate with band members in one room by banging on pipes in the adjoining storage room. When someone goes to check, there's no one there.

The other ghostly presence is said to be felt in the bathroom. The presence is so creepy, it makes students leave the room instead of doing their business.

Washington High School is located at 1700 Klatt Road.

City 75: Oshkosh

Grand Opera House

Beautiful on the outside, beautiful *and* haunted on the inside—at least if you believe the stories that continue to be told about this landmark located at 100 High Avenue.

Grand Opera House, Oshkosh.

The lovely facility, now owned by the City of Oshkosh, opened its doors in 1883. The history of the place is incredible: Susan B. Anthony, Charlie Chaplin, Mark Twain, the Marx Brothers, and Harry Houdini have all held performances or speeches here.

Like many old buildings, it went through a period of decline; at one point, it showed X-rated films. When restoration work began in the 1970s, people began reporting ghost sightings. Some believe they see the ghost of a former stage manager. Others insist they see a woman who is dressed in flapper-era clothing. One of the most common sightings is of a ghost dog that roams the opera house.

Today, in addition to seeing a ghost dog or people dressed in nineteenth-century clothing, you might see another strange occurrence. One seat in the first or second row of the theater will be down when all the other seats in the place are up. This seat is supposedly where the stage manager, Percy Keene, who died in 1967, used to sit. The same stage manager has also been seen standing in

110

the balcony, looking down at a film crew with a friendly smile. Former employees have reported hearing footsteps walking by when no one is there.

This site is unusual in that the Opera House is proud of their ghosts. In October, it is transformed into A Theater of Lost Souls (see Attractions section). During the rest of the year, you may take a tour that is well worth your time.

New Moon Café

This building, located at 401 Main Street, was originally called the Beckwith. It was destroyed by a fire in 1875. Ghosts from this time period are said to haunt the building, though the ghosts could not be from the fire, as no one is believed to have died in the fire.

Someone, however, did die in the building five years later. Her name was Mrs. Simon Paige, and she was said to be a wealthy lumberman's wife.

When people are in the café on a quiet day, their premium cup of coffee may not be the only thing to get their heart pumping. Ghosts of a wealthy woman believed to be Mrs. Paige, a young boy, and a bellhop have all been spotted here.

New Moon Café, Oshkosh.

Paine Art Center, Oshkosh.

Paine Art Center

At least one ghost is said to be a permanent resident of this historic site, and this particular ghost is said to have a fondness for rearranging furniture. One can only imagine how busy it is—the Paine, an English Tudor, has forty-seven rooms.

Lumber tycoon Nathan Paine, the man the estate is named after, kept journals. These journals are said to get leafed through by invisible hands. Mr. Paine or just a nosy unnamed ghost? Could be either. Maybe neither. You see, Mr. Paine never lived here. He and his wife completed the mansion during the Great Depression. Rumor has it that bitter, and dare I say jealous, residents of Oshkosh threatened to kill the couple if they ever moved in. Another story is that a worker threatened to burn down the estate if the Paines ever moved in. Why all this anger? Well, it seems Mr. and Mrs. Paine paid their employees with vouchers that they could spend at stores they owned, not with cash.

No matter which story is true, the Paines wound up donating the estate to the city.

A woman ghost is said to sometimes join a tour group. She will invariably be at the back of the group and will start talking about things inside the house. When people turn around to see the source of the voice, the woman disappears.

Other ghostly sightings feature Edward or George Paine, who were the grandfather and father of Nathan Paine.

The Paine Art Center is located at 1410 Algoma Boulevard.

Riverside Cemetery

I visited the cemetery in January and was reminded of a well-laid out city with all its street signs. However, when you reach the back of the cemetery, you can see across a beautiful "wild" area, and houses not far away.

The stones and crypts inside the cemetery are among some of most unique I've ever seen. One University of Wisconsin-Oshkosh student said the area around the crypts is said to be the most haunted spot in the cemetery. She said the area around a tall woman monument and a man with a rifle at the rear of the cemetery are also spots where ghostly apparitions have been seen at night as well as during the daytime.

Riverside Cemetery, Oshkosh.

While the student has heard numerous reports of children ghosts in the cemetery that disappear, she and her friends have only seen adult-sized shadows and mists.

The stories of children ghosts—especially a young girl ghost that disappears when you look directly at her—and a story of children racing around the cemetery as if playing tag are the most often associated with this cemetery.

I was warned not to visit this cemetery, located at 1901 Algoma Boulevard, at night alone.

Friend's Unique Boutique

This unique store formerly known as Starseed and located at 457 North Main Street in an old brick building, has your usual ghostly goings-on: Lights go on and off by themselves, and footsteps can be heard going up and down the stairs when there are no humans around. But that's not all...

A young child is believed to haunt the building. She was killed after an accidental fall down the stairs. A ghostly cat, perhaps the little girl's, has also been seen wandering the building.

City 76: Pipe

Capone's

Built in the early 1900s, this building, more commonly known as Club Harbor, was a bed and breakfast in its early days. It was also once called Fuhrman's Hotel. It was added to the National Register of Historical Places in 1980 and is located at the corner of Highway 151 and County W at N 10302 Hwy 151.

At least two murders and a suicide are said to have occurred here. Incredibly, all of them were said to have taken place in the same third-story room. Even today, if you look up at this room, you can sometimes see the ghost of a woman who died there. The woman has blonde hair, or appears as a white figure.

City 77: Plover

Club Forest

This historic bar, located between Wisconsin Rapids and Plover, is proud of its resident ghost, Melvin. He lived here during the days when Club Forest was visited by Al Capone and was a house of "ill repute."

Club Forest, Plover.

Club Forest got its beginnings in 1927, as a small railroad stop tavern. Co-owner Pam Booth says Melvin, a black man, was brought to the area from Chicago by former owners to pick up women from the train station, which was two blocks away on the corner of County F and Highway 54. It was Melvin's job to watch over the ladies.

Pam Booth says she and others who work and visit the bar love having Melvin around; he's a friendly and protective presence. Pam says she was once staying in the small living quarters at the bar and was robbed not once, but twice, by the same young man. Strangely—or maybe not—the burglar never entered the room she was in (which happened to be where the bar's money was also temporarily being kept). She even had a $20 bill on the dresser on one occasion. Melvin keeping an eye on her and the bar?

She remembers a number of other things happening in the bar that can't be explained by conventional methods. She notes that these

115

paranormal activities seem to increase in the fall of the year. While strange things usually occur when only a few people are present, sometimes the entire bar is treated to an experience.

During a Packers game last year, the jukebox, which had been turned off so the speakers could be utilized for the game on TV, suddenly blasted on. "Oh my God, Melvin's here!" people in the bar yelled.

The dartboard and jukebox also turn on by themselves, and the jukebox is only a couple months old. Pam remembers, "One time, a really eerie song started playing. It was something I'd never heard before, like mystical piano music. We checked to see what the song was, but it doesn't exist."

Kevin, a Club Forest employee, didn't believe in ghosts until he had an experience of his own. Pam says he was taking out the garbage and heard women laughing near the pavilion. Thinking maybe someone was back there, he checked it out, but found no one anywhere. He got rid of the garbage, turned around, and headed back. That's when he heard footsteps behind him. Kevin ran to his car, got in, and left the premises.

Pam has experienced other things such as hearing the sound of someone pounding their beer can on the bar (they served only canned beer in the 1990s) when she was alone, and seeing a bar stool shoot across the room—which has happened not only to her, but other people on different occasions.

So why is Melvin a part of the Club Forest scene? He was believed to have fallen in love with one of the prostitutes. When one man got too rough with her, Melvin got in fight that ended with his death.

A local paranormal group investigated the club and came away with compelling evidence that the bar is indeed haunted—something many already believe.

Stop by for great food, a fantastic atmosphere, and a cool ghost. Club Forest is located at 1176 Club Forest Drive.

Cottage House Restaurant

This beautiful old building, which is more than 125 years old, was first a private residence and then a restaurant. Before the Cottage House Restaurant was called the Cottage House, it was known as the Old Sherman House. It was named after Eugene Sherman, one of Plover's most respected and admired residents.

No one has any information about the early years of the building to suggest that goings-on were anything other than normal. It wasn't until the Sowiak family lived there that any ghostly activity was known

Cottage House Restaurant, Plover.

to have happened. The Sowiaks lived there from the late 1950s to the early 1980s. During that time, no one knew what went on behind closed doors either, because the family didn't talk about it. Later, a Sowiak family member said a host of paranormal events occurred while the family lived there.

The next owners decided to turn the building into a restaurant. They went about renovations without realizing they had a ghost or ghosts in the building. It wasn't until they opened their restaurant, which they called the Old Sherman House, that they realized something otherworldly shared the building with them and their customers.

During the time the Old Sherman House was in business, employees said they felt invisible shapes moving past them in some of the rooms. Not only that—plates and glasses would fly off the counters and bar and actually burst in front of employees and customers. Windows made of glass would shatter, doors would open and shut by themselves, and lights in the restaurant would not work properly.

While a baby was the only one believed to have died in the building, many of the former owners were strict Methodists, who disapproved of alcohol. A church deacon lived in the house from 1903 to 1945, and some believe the deacon was offended that his former home was now selling spirits.

The owners kept the Old Sherman House open for a few years, but the ghost in the building was eventually said to drive them from the building. It was opened again later as the Cottage House Restaurant. Stories still circulated about the sounds of a baby crying and sometimes an apparition in the upstairs windows, but no frightening episodes have been reported.

Unfortunately, the restaurant, which was known for its excellent cuisine and atmosphere, is now for sale. The last time I drove past, "Price Reduced" had been added to the "For Sale" sign in front of the building. It's in a prime location. It has a wonderful reputation. Is its ghostly past keeping prospective buyers away?

City 78: Readfield

Readfield Graveyard

This final resting place is also known as the Evangelical Lutheran Zion's Cemetery and is said to have one grave in particular that is haunted. The name on the large monument is "Nahring."

Readfield Graveyard is located on County W, just north of town. The polished marble ball top of the monument is said to swivel during the full moon. It is supposedly guided by the spirit of the man the stone is named for.

The story is well-known in the area, but no one I spoke to has actually seen the marble top swivel.

City 79: River Falls

Parker Mansion

This notoriously haunted mansion, with its eye-catching cupola atop the building, is located at 315 Maple Street. It was built by Colonel Charles Parker, an early Wisconsin lieutenant governor, as a single-family home. It is currently a multi-apartment dwelling.

Former students who lived here have reported electrical troubles such as lights flicking on and off and stereo problems. While you might be able to chalk these things up to electrical or wiring problems, there are other things, like doors opening on their own, that you can't.

A poltergeist is said to inhabit the building—this is a mischievous ghost that can be heard but not seen. In this case, maybe it's a good thing.

UW-River Falls

While many students say they've felt a presence near them on campus when they've been alone, one professor had a distinct experience.

The ghost said to haunt UW-River Falls is believed to be that of Sanford Syse, a former speech professor. Syse designed the Blanche Davis Theatre; he also paid a visit to Professor Jim Zimmerman one summer night.

As Zimmerman was writing notes while finishing a rehearsal, he looked up and saw a man dressed in a red T-shirt and jeans walking to the center of stage. He asked the man if he needed anything; before he got an answer, the man disappeared. Zimmerman was told the man was Syse, who died in 1973.

UW-River Falls is located at 410 South 3rd Street.

City 80: Rock Island

Rock Island State Park

If you want to see the ghost of Rock Island, you're going to have to take the Rock Island Ferry from Washington Island. From there, you'll have to hoof it; there are no vehicles or bicycles allowed here.

Former lighthouse keeper, David E. Corbin, is said to haunt the Potawatomi Lighthouse. He was the first keeper of the Potawatomi Light. He died in December of 1852, and was said to have died a lonely man. (He once left the island for two weeks to find a wife, but returned empty-handed.)

The first lighthouse was built in 1836, before Wisconsin was officially a state. When it was destroyed in the 1850s, the current one was built in 1858. Besides being haunted, it's a really cool place to visit because of its richly preserved history, and it's on the National Register of Historic Places.

The graveyard near the lighthouse is said to be where apparitions have been spotted and cold spots have been experienced.

City 81: Rosendale

Callan Road

This road is best known as Witch Road because of the witch who haunts it. Which begs the question: How did the witch die? If you drive down the road at certain times, you may decide the smell killed her. I've been down this allegedly haunted road twice and both times I thought the smell would implode my lungs. The road has houses on each end, and forested areas and crops in the middle. At one place, there's a slough area. And in that slough area is the smell that really is worse than death. But getting back to the story…

A witch lived on Callan Road years ago, hence the name Witch Road. But she's not the only one no longer breathing that's said to haunt the road. A little girl in white has been seen among the trees at road's edge.

The trees themselves are a strange sight during the times of the year they don't have leaves. The branches are misshapen and gnarled; they seem twisted into impossible shapes. Whitish lights have been seen in the trees. The witch is said to be responsible.

Some say the road is blacker and colder than it should be on some nights. This is meant to be a warning to go back the way you came and leave the road to those it belongs to.

The road is actually closer to Ripon than Rosendale and is located in the town of Metomen, in Fond du Lac County.

City 82: St. Nazianz

JFK Prep

This is one of the most investigated—by amateurs and professionals—haunted sites in Wisconsin. Some who have visited recently say they captured nothing out of the ordinary on audio or video; others have left with both.

One explanation for this level of disparity can be explained by a former student. He said that if you believe in spirits and a higher power, you will be aware of the spiritual presences still there; they will make themselves known as benevolent. If you come to the old school to scare someone or to destroy property, you can bet you will met with something that will try to deter you from your mischief.

Before I get too far into the story—the buildings of St. Nazianz are all privately owned. This means NO TRESPASSING, and this rule is strictly enforced in this town.

Like all places that have "strangeness" attached to them, some say it's definitely haunted; some say it just has a creepy past. A nun ghost, priest ghost, boy ghosts, and girl ghost are all said to call the prep home.

Let's start with a little history—always the best way to understand the present. This place was once a Salvatorian Seminary. Young men came here to train for priesthood or the ministry; so right off the bat it's unlikely that nuns would teach them.

A girl was said to have hung herself here in the 1970s. This may be true, but I have not seen documentation. Other stories of young men who committed suicide each Lenten season are also told; these are believed to be fact.

There is a crypt on the grounds near the Loretto Shrine containing the body of founder, Reverend Ambrose Oschwald. Graves of fellow priests, now said to be in terrible shape, are close by. Some have reported seeing the graves rise and sink. This may be true, but I'm guessing it's a slow process of rising and sinking taking place over many years; not seconds.

There are stories of people getting caught in the tunnels. Again, this is possible just because tunnels, and lots of 'em, do exist on this sprawling property.

Speaking of sprawling property; the area called JFK Prep consists of a church, school, cemetery (now owned by the historical society), garage, printing building, steam tunnels, boiler room, and a forest…and these are just a few of my favorite things.

A dirt road circles the property. One building owner held "haunted" tours several years ago to help raise money for renovation of his property. If the building owner believes his property is haunted, who's to say we shouldn't? Many are happy the beautiful old structures are being restored. It's a shame to see history neglected and destroyed.

City 83: Shawano County

Chicken Alley

This Shawano County road near the Outagamie County line, is located not far from the tiny town of Rose Lawn. Chicken Alley is actually the top part of French Road. I found no history on how it got its name, but Chicken Alley does have two ghost stories associated with it.

The first story deals with a paranormal light you believe is a snowmobile chasing you. No matter how fast you travel, this persistent light will never catch up to you. Good thing, because you will need to travel through a haunted forest to try to escape it.

The other story deals with chickens—literally. On nights with a full moon, you are able to see the outline of a large spooky tree and wild chickens running around. Strange. Even stranger that you can see right through the chickens. But don't get out of your car to investigate the ghost chickens. I've heard a variety of consequence stories; none of them are good.

City 84: Sherwood

High Cliff State Park

This park is the only state-owned recreational area on Lake Winnebago. Although High Cliff, the third largest park in Wisconsin, is known for its campsites and trails, it is also known by some for being haunted. Experiences here range from feeling warm and having cold breezes blow through your body in various places in the park, to seeing misty apparitions on trails and near the cliff.

The park is named High Cliff for the limestone cliff of the Niagara Escarpment, which parallels the east shore of Lake Winnebago.

Perhaps the spiritual presence has more to do with an archeological feature of the park—its effigy mounds. Roving Siouan Indians built effigy mounds in what is now the park between 1,000 and 1,500 years ago, including four panther-shaped mounds, two buffalo-shaped mounds, conical mounds, and a linear mound. The park also contains a breathtaking twelve-foot statue of Winnebago Indian Chief Red Bird which stands on a huge granite rock. Some believe his spirit watches over the park.

The park's address is N7630 State Park Road.

City 85: Sparta

Boys & Girls Club

This story and the next story about the Wisconsin Child Center Cemetery have something in common: The Boys & Girls Club in Sparta was at one time the Wisconsin Child Center.

Now the Boys & Girls Club building is home to an annual haunted house called appropriately enough, House of Shadows. This haunted house is extra special because it's haunted in real life. Some get chills when they're alone in the building. Others say they hear the faint laughter of children as well as crying when they're in the building. Numerous photos taken inside the building have produced orbs, white shadows, and streaks.

The Boys & Girls Club is located just down the street from the Sparta Public Golf Course, home of the Wisconsin Child Center Cemetery. You can stop by the building for a screaming good time this Halloween. It's located at 1000 East Montgomery Avenue.

"No golf carts in the cemetery please!" Wisconsin Child Cemetery, Sparta.

Wisconsin Child Center Cemetery

Fore! Huh?

Incredibly, this haunted cemetery is smack dab in the middle of the Sparta Public Golf Course.

If you look between the greens and see the bright white fence in front of gorgeous landscaping, you might think there's some kind of park inside the course. It isn't until you get close to the gate that you see the lilac-draped sign that tells you nicely, "No golf carts in cemetery please."

On the inside of the fence, you are struck by the stark contrast of the tiny headstones. There are 305 unclaimed children buried here. Most of the deaths are attributed to epidemics such as diphtheria and scarlet fever. No names are on the mossy, old stones, but there is a nice monument on one side of the cemetery that lists all the children buried there along with the corresponding headstone.

Many visitors to the cemetery at dusk or later have heard childish voices; some have seen ghosts—mostly girls. White shadows have also been seen in the cemetery after dark.

City 86: Stevens Point

Calvin Blood Cemetery

Blood Cemetery is the name thrill seekers use when they talk about this cemetery. It is also known as Woodville Cemetery and Linwood Cemetery. The latter is because the cemetery is in the township of Linwood.

The cemetery is located on Cemetery Road off West River Drive. Locals don't want you to go there, so if you do, consider yourself a bug under a microscope. The fence of this teeny-tiny cemetery is posted with warnings. "No Trespassing" and a Neighborhood Watch sign are the first things that catch your eye when you approach the cemetery. They seem to say "Nice to see you!" Not.

Farmland is all around the cemetery. Cars were parked at a nearby farm when I stopped by, and although people weren't visible, I couldn't help but feel that even though you couldn't see them, they could definitely see you.

Then why is this cemetery the stuff that legends are made of? Good question. There are very few bodies in this cemetery, so the word

Calvin Blood Cemetery, Stevens Point.

124

Calvin Blood marker.

"Blood" must be the draw. Stories have been circulating for years that the cemetery is haunted—and people with psychic abilities and those sensitive to spirits say it's true. Paranormal investigators, however, disagree. In fact, the Paranormal Assessment Team, or P.A.T., put out a letter saying the cemetery was investigated and was declared not haunted.

The debate rages on, but the story about the cemetery is not debatable. The land the cemetery sits on was donated for use as a cemetery in the late 1800s so that people with no money could bury their loved ones. This plot of land was named the Woodville Cemetery.

Calvin Blood was born in 1825. Apparently, the poor boy got picked on a lot because of his name. Then came the Civil War; he joined the Union Army, was given an honorable discharge at the end of the war, moved back to the area, and then married. He, his wife, and family farmed in the area. He died when he was eighty-two years old of consumption. End of Calvin Blood's life, but hardly the end of the story.

125

Somewhere along the line, a different story began circulating that is wildly different than the true version. In this story, when Mr. Blood returned from the war, some of his former friends came to town looking for him. When they found him, they chopped off his legs and left him to bleed to death. He was said to have died on the property where his body was laid to rest.

It's said that if you visit the cemetery, you'll see a legless Mr. Blood hobbling toward you. But don't worry, he's not out for your blood; he just wants to find his former friends who chopped off his legs—he has nothing against you or me.

The story also says that if you are at the cemetery and break a branch off a tree near the grave, you will be cursed for life. No reason. You'll just be cursed.

I didn't touch a thing when I was at the cemetery. Oddly, though, there was one dead branch near Calvin Blood's marker when I got there...

West Scott Street Home

This story comes from a woman who spent her childhood in Stevens Point.

"Hi, I am Michelle Laucke and I believe in ghosts. Why? Because I've seen them, I've felt them, and I know they are around us.

"My first encounter was when I was about five years old. The woman was young, probably in her twenties; she had long blond hair and a billowy old-fashioned night dress that went to the floor, and she wasn't alone. At her side was a German Shepherd dog—the brown kind, not the all black. One might wonder how I knew they were ghosts and my answer is simple: I could see through them. "To a five-year-old, this entity wasn't the least bit scary, she had a dog and was beautiful. In fact, I called out to her to stop as I wanted to pet the dog. I was on the first floor of my old bedroom which had old hardwood floors and a narrow staircase leading to the attic. She looked at me when I called out and just smiled, and she and the dog seemed to float up the stair case. I called out again and my mom came to the room and told me to hush, I was just having a dream. But I know it wasn't, because if it was a dream, why do I still remember it perfectly clear to this day? And she came often in my childhood, I just didn't tell Mom. The house, still standing, is located on Scott Street."

The two-story home is located near the end of the road, close to the train tracks.

City 87: Stockbridge

Joe Road

Part legend, part ghost story, this is one place to put on your to-visit list. The story begins in the early 1900s. The state of Wisconsin wanted to put a road through the area, which would run across Native American burial grounds. The groundskeeper, a man called Indian Joe, refused and was run over and killed. While this may or not be an actual event, the state of Wisconsin did build Joe Road.

Joe Road is listed as a gravity hill, but those who live near the road and those who have traveled it say that more than gravity is involved; they believe one particular stretch of the road is haunted. First, there's a hill, then a flat spot, then another hill. Some say if you put baby powder on the back of your car, put your car in neutral, and take your foot off the gas pedal or the brake, Indian Joe will push you up the hill to the end of the road. You can tell because there are handprints in the baby powder.

There are just as many, however, that say they didn't have handprints in the baby powder on the back of their car, but the car did move to the end of the road on its own—no ghostly helping hands involved.

City 88: Sturgeon Bay

Memories of a Sturgeon Bay Home

This comes from Wisconsin author, Ruth Forrest Glenn.

In 1990, I had the experience of living in Sturgeon Bay, Wisconsin, often traveling to the end of the peninsula to Baileys Harbor and such.

It was around this time that a graveyard was uncovered in a construction project for area tourists. In the study of the remains, it is believed that this cemetery was linked to Harriet Tubman and the slave underground, and that it was the first cemetery to be found that had the remains of some slaves that didn't live once they reached freedom. The construction company and the historical society worked together to preserve this cemetery, marking it off as undeveloped land. I had bought an old house that seemed to carry the bay town's history with it. After living in the old house a couple of months, I felt an unnerving feeling late one night that would continue to wake me from my slumber the entire time I lived there.

There was an old walled-in staircase to the two upstairs rooms. They seemed dark and almost hidden in themselves. If anything knocked against the wall, like furniture or things taken upstairs, the sound was hollow. The walls echoed. They seemed to have been boarded, painted, and wallpapered over to an extreme. This began to perplex my thoughts, so I put a living room chair on the left side of the stairway opening from the living room. Then I placed my computer desk and chair on the right side. I hadn't seen anything tangible in spirit as of yet, working late as I often did. I went to go to bed about 1 am, checked the doors of the house to make sure they were locked, and fell asleep. At 3 am, I was awakened to a soft humming sound. It seemed to come from the living room. Startled and drowsy, I walked into the living room. The soft chair I had placed on the left side of the stairway had a luminous-looking little old lady with silver hair in it. She was knitting something and humming. I stood still in amazement, just watching her continue her task. In an instant, she vanished. I checked the doors of the house and all was locked just as I had left them when I went to bed. The woman continued to make her presence known for most of the time I lived there. I wanted to know what she was doing there or how her aura tied into the house. I would also hear walking and whispering upstairs in the house, though it was only a storage area to me. As I researched the history of Sturgeon Bay and the house, I believe I found my answer when the cemetery found a couple of years before came up in the old microfilm at the library.

I was amazed to learn that there was a secret room built into the walls of the house's stairway. It was a hiding place for the Underground Railroad and those who ran toward freedom. The hollow walls were no longer a mystery. I felt compassion for those who lived and died trying to find an escape from one of our country's hardest trials of time. The lady still made an appearance in the soft chair, humming from time to time, as I lived in the house. This gave me the spiritual impression that some of the spirits involved with the house's earlier days had found a sense of peace and belonging.

Sherwood Point Lighthouse

This lighthouse, built in 1883 and operated by personnel until 1983, was the last lighthouse on the Great Lakes to be converted to automation. It's now a private retreat house for Coast Guard personnel and is open for tours to the public during a very narrow timeframe: the third week in May.

If you are lucky enough to take a tour of the lighthouse, you may just hear the stories about a woman who supposedly haunts the lighthouse. Odd occurrences are logged by people who stay there; many report odd noises and the feeling you are not alone.

The ghostly presence may be that of Minnie Cochems. She and her husband, William, operated the lighthouse in both the nineteenth and twentieth centuries. She, her husband, and their children are remembered for keeping the lighthouse grounds in immaculate condition. Mrs. Cochems climbed out of bed on August 17, 1928, collapsed, and then died. The lighthouse displays a plaque to her memory even today. She is said to move things around and be responsible for cold spots in the lighthouse.

City 89: Tomah

Buckley Park

The park, located on East Holton Street, looks like an average park—only it isn't. A ghost is said to walk slowly alongside the trail, past the bench. If you look at it and do nothing else, it will continue walking. If you are startled by its see-through appearance and make noise, it will immediately vanish into thin air.

Most of the ghost's appearances have been near sunset. Cold breezes have been reported here, even when the air is calm and warm.

City 90: Waupaca

Cristy Mansion

This beautiful haunted house has private owners and they aren't the people who reported the paranormal activity, so please respect their privacy. No one is sure if the house is still haunted, but even if it isn't, the former ghostly activities that took place there are definitely worth mentioning.

The 1890s Queen Ann-style mansion located on Lake Street was built by Calib Shearer, an attorney and lumberman, but it is called the Cristy Mansion after the Joseph T. Cristy family that lived there from 1907-1967, and owned the mansion until 1981. The enormous house with two turrets and a carriage house was apparently haunted even before the Cristys moved in.

In fact, the same night Mrs. Cristy and her three children moved in, she heard horses whinnying outside even though there were no living horses anywhere around the mansion. Unbeknownst to her at that time, ponies used to be kept in the carriage house at the rear of the house.

The next morning, a window shade came down on Mrs. Cristy. Adding insult to injury, the sound of a male's sharp laughter rang out behind her. There was no one there—that she could see anyway. That same day, her daughter's glasses were knocked from her face, shattering one of the lenses. The girl's brother witnessed the event. The two children fled the area, terrified.

The family began to become used to the sound of footsteps throughout the house. Mrs. Cristy was also once enveloped by a freezing draft of air. She kept it from her children, as she mostly likely did with most untoward things; she didn't want to frighten them.

Amazingly, the family began to interact with the entities in the house as they became accepting of each others' existence.

Simpson's Restaurant

Simpson's looks like an ordinary restaurant, but some insist it is anything but ordinary. Why? Because an entire family is said to haunt this establishment.

Simpson's Restaurant, Waupaca.

Maybe the family of ghosts said to haunt the restaurant likes the ambience, or maybe it's the great food. Regardless, this unnamed family is to said to make their presence known during the nighttime hours. But don't come in for dinner hoping to witness ghostly shenanigans. Simpson's ghosts do "hang around," but don't cause trouble.

Employees and regular patrons of the restaurant are said to have seen this family walking around, going about their business as if they didn't know anyone else was there—signs that this is a residual haunting.

I spoke to a number of Waupaca residents who said they had heard there were "nice" ghosts at Simpsons, but didn't know anything more than that. The restaurant is located at 222 Main Street.

City 91: Wautoma

Poltergeist in Wautoma Home

This story comes from someone who has heard stories of this haunted house from a very credible source: her father, Tom. She says: "There is a house near the corner of State Road 21 and County Road II outside of Wautoma." This stretch of road is between Wautoma and Richford. She doesn't know who lives there now, but when her dad lived there when he was younger, he knew something ghostly lived there with him because it was always making noises and moving things around on him.

"He never wanted to believe it," Tom's daughter says. "Then one night he said he was sitting on his bed, facing the door to the living room, and he heard it. He got up to check out what the noise was and all he saw was that his high school picture was turned facing the wall. He said he didn't think anything of it; he thought one of his friends did it early that night. Well, he turned it facing him and went to the kitchen, and when he came back, it was turned facing the wall again. He thought his friends were still there screwing with him."

She says he flipped it around again and went into his bedroom, sat down on the bed and waited until he heard something, so he could catch them in the act. "While he waited, he was thinking that it was definitely a ghost. All of a sudden, the wooden rocking chair started rocking. He said it rocked almost violently, as if someone was sitting in it and pushing really hard with their legs. He freaked out, but ran over to it to stop it. When he turned around, the picture was turned around again. He booked it for the door and slept at his parents' house that night in his truck. He moved out that next day and never spent another night there."

She says her father knows now that it was a demon ghost playing tricks. But the people who lived there after him thought it was funny that there was a ghost living with them and they even named it.

She says, "My dad doesn't think it's funny because that is a real demon and that's what it wants, to distract them from the truth." She told me she got goose bumps just remembering the story.

City 92: West Salem

Garland Homestead

In the 1970s, the Garland homestead that once belonged to Pulitzer Prize-winning author Hamlin Garland, began undergoing remodeling to get it back to its original shape.

That's when a ghost began making its presence known. Lights came on at will, thermostats turned up, and other objects moved on their own, even after the house was checked and locked up. Most of the odd occurrences have been recorded, but there really is no pattern to them.

One event was particularly disturbing. One morning, after the house was opened, the form of a person was found pressed into the covers of the bed in Garland's bedroom. Not a single other thing was amiss. It was as if a body had been placed on the bed, then lifted off. The covers were not otherwise disturbed. No one had been left in that building and the doors had been locked.

Some say the ghost responsible is Garland himself. Could be. Though he didn't die at the homestead, it's said he wanted his ashes to be brought to West Salem and scattered on the hillside.

As we all know, what you want and what you get are sometimes two different things. Garland was brought back to Wisconsin, but his ashes are buried beside his parents in the Neshonoc Cemetery. Close to where he wanted his ashes, but maybe not close enough. The homestead is located at 357 West Garland Street.

City 93: Weyauwega

Marsh Road

Even if I didn't see anything paranormal while I was here, there is something about this road even in the daytime, that gave me the creeps despite the beauty of the area. There are a number of videos posted on the Internet by intrepid ghost hunters who have traveled the road at night, who have had varying experiences. There are just as many stories about the road.

The best known story features the Goatman, who is said to take matters into his own hands—or cloven hooves—to make sure teens

Marsh Road, Weyauwega.

in the area behave themselves. In the 1960s or 1970s, a couch was located halfway down the road that had a reputation as a make-out couch. One evening, the Goatman stumbled across a couple making out and killed them. Sometimes, the Goatman is the ghost that haunts the road; sometimes, the story has the unfortunate couple doing the haunting.

The second story features a place-shifting aspect that I can attest to. Some say the road never seems to end. Others say it feels extraordinary long traveling in one direction, but very short going in the other direction. When I was traveling down the dirt road section of Marsh Road, it felt creepier the longer I drove. I finally felt compelled to turn around a little past the creek and quickly headed back the way I came. I was on Highway 10 for a good five minutes before I felt back to normal.

Another story attributed to this road is one that features a young couple in a car who was driving down Marsh Road. Some say the event happened during the day; say it was night. All stories agree that a semi (truck) was in a driveway on that road and chose that moment to reverse. The young couple didn't have time to stop and were killed. Decapitated, actually. Now, at night when you are driving down Marsh Road and see headlights, it very well may be the young, and dead, couple heading toward you. Only the lights never reach you. You will seem to drive for miles and never meet or pass the headlights.

Other amateur investigators have reported having children's handprints on the back of their cars after driving down this road and seeing ghostly children in their rear view mirror.

City 94: Whitehall

Oak Park Inn

Her name is Ida May. And even if you've never heard of her, you just might see her ghost if you drive past the property or stay at this beautiful inn. The story of the young slave who befriended Wisconsin soldiers during the Civil War and became a part of a local family (the Hopkins) is not well-known despite the fact that Ida May was laid to rest on the family property.

Her gravesite is in the rear formal garden of the inn, located at18224 Ervin Street. Her presence is peaceful. Guests who stay at the inn and visit the garden say it's one of the most serene spots they've ever been.

Those that see Ida May never feel frightened or disturbed.

City 95: Whitelaw

Maplecrest Sanitarium

It's abandoned and it's creepy, so it shouldn't be a surprise that people say it's very haunted. In the 1930s, it was a tuberculosis hospital; after that, it was a sanitarium until it closed.

The rundown white building, also known as Whitelaw Sanitarium has three wings and three stories and is partially hidden by woods a mile north of the city of Whitelaw. If you're not sure you're in the right area, the rusty water tower is a dead giveaway.

From the outside, you might see people staring at you from third floor windows—many say that's the best place to see a ghostly figure or face. If you somehow get inside the building, you might hear the thin sound of laughter, or have a door slam next to you.

The sanitarium is on Preston Road. A two-story building next to the sanitarium is currently being used as an apartment building. No one has come forward with stories about ghosts in the building.

Warning: The driveway and all the property is private. No trespassing.

City 96: Wild Rose

Tuttle Lake

This lake is located in Waushara County on Tuttle Lake Road and is the subject of at least two ghostly legends. The best known legend centers around a farmer who owned this land. He found out his wife was pregnant and drowned her. Ever hear of adoption?! In any event, after he drowned his wife, the farmer disappeared. Since then, a ghostly woman has been spotted in the lake; sometimes she's trying to swim to shore, sometimes she's floating lifelessly.

Moving to the second "haunting" story. The property owned by the farmer is now a campsite. There have been some really unnerving experiences by campers. Some have run from blinding lights only to find themselves in places that are physically impossible. They say these experiences are all tied to the drowned woman. It is said that her body was discovered in the lake and buried on the property.

I know people who have spent time here overnight. They haven't seen anything ghostly or paranormal, but several times they've heard sounds that are very like someone desperately stroking toward shore. When they race to check it out, there's no one there.

City 97: Wisconsin Rapids

CD's Pub and Grill

Shadow figures and disembodied voices are just a couple of things that have been reported inside this building.

The pub and grill, located at 2650 Plover Road on the outskirts of Wisconsin Rapids, also features more disturbing paranormal activities. The feeling of being touched and then being surrounded by the strong smell of cigar smoke, even though no one is smoking a cigar, are a couple things you might experience there.

Events such as the TV turning on and off and the channels changing by themselves has been caught on video and audio. No word on the identity of the ghost or ghosts. Guesses include former customers and a former owner.

Forest Hill Cemetery

This cemetery, located at 631 Spring Street, looks like many other cemeteries. One thing that sets it apart, however, is the sound of babies

CD's Pub and Grill, Wisconsin Rapids.

crying in the baby section of the cemetery when there are no living babies around.

Others have heard someone faintly calling their names when they've been alone. This is said to happen during the day and at night.

A story about a monument at the top of the hill that causes machine failure is another story associated with Forest Hill. When I visited the cemetery, I didn't experience any camera or machine problems.

Many of Wisconsin Rapids most well-respected citizens are buried here. Among them: the Mead family, whose markers include one incredible monument.

Hotel Mead

This building catches your attention when you go downtown. It's big, it's beautiful, and according to many—it's haunted. The biggest presence is said to be associated with the Shanghai Room. The ghost is of a female employee who was brutally murdered there in 1953. Today, lights flicker, doors shut by themselves, and the smell of blood is evident within twenty feet of this room. This room is unusually cold.

The hotel, located at 451 East Grand Avenue, is also said to be haunted by other entities. I recently spoke to a woman who works at the Mead Hotel; she said she has never had any ghostly experiences in the Shanghai Room, but she's been upstairs working in a dining room with one or two other people, and chairs would move on their own, away from the tables. She said no one was near the chairs or could have moved them. While she isn't sure she believes in ghosts or spirits, she admits she and the others in the room thought this was "really strange."

Other employees have heard men talking in one of the men's rest rooms when the no one was around. When they went to see what was going on, there was no one inside.

There have also been reports of people talking inside empty rooms and employees have also heard the jingle of keys right next to them when they were alone.

I also spoke with someone else who has knowledge of the hotel. She said she and other employees do whatever it takes to not be alone in the Shanghai Room. She says the stories about a ghost in the Shanghai Room are way more than just a story. She says the ghostly presence is downright frightening. It has "pushed" her out of the room along with an icy breeze that was so cold, it hurt her skin.

House on 12th Avenue

The owners of this small house less than a block from the train tracks don't wish to have their address listed. One daughter who has lived in this house from the time she was born until she was an adult, has had experiences with the little girl ghost that lives in the house with the family.

Friends who stayed overnight sometimes couldn't make it the entire night because they were so frightened. The sound of footsteps up and down the stairs, as well as physically seeing the little girl ghost were usually enough to not only make a believer out of the guest, but to also send them racing out of the house.

The little girl ghost is like any normal girl. She can sometimes be heard crying. She also tugs on the clothing of the living as if to get their attention.

Interview with Andrew Kirkpatrick

Andrew Kirkpatrick, a UW-Stevens Point student with a double major in broadfield social-science/history, and secretary of Wisconsin Rapids Everything X-treme Ink, recently spoke to me about his paranormal experiences in the Wisconsin Rapids area.

St. Joseph Catholic Cemetery, Seneca.

St. Joseph Catholic Cemetery

Kirkpatrick has visited St. Joseph Catholic Cemetery, located on County D in the town of Seneca between Wisconsin Rapids and Pittsville several times. An old white church is located in front of the cemetery which brackets the church on the south and west. A brick, two-story house and small parking area lie on the other side of the street directly across from the church and cemetery.

One of the most memorable visits include seeing a man leaning on a monument at this cemetery as he and one of his friends flashed their flashlights across the stone. Incredibly, this isn't the most unnerving thing to happen there. Kirkpatrick remembers one time he went to the cemetery with a group of friends. They drove there in two cars, then he and a friend hopped in one car and the rest of the group stayed back about a half mile.

Kirkpatrick says, "We left a voice recorder on the top of a tombstone next to the church, facing the road." They turned on the recorder, hopped back in the car, and joined the rest of their friends. About thirty minutes later, they returned to the cemetery. "As we walked to the tombstone, my friend, Canaan, said we weren't going to get anything." Turns out he was wrong. "The first thing we saw was the voice recorder wasn't facing the road like we'd left it."

Next, they played back what they had recorded. "About ten seconds before Canaan told me that we weren't going to get anything, we heard this scratchy noise, like the voice recorder was physically being turned around on the tombstone." Neither Kirkpatrick or his friend had touched it since placing it on the tombstone facing the road. He says, "We also saw no one move the recorder as the sound of the recorder moving occurred only seconds before we walked up to it."

On a different trip to the cemetery, Kirkpatrick and a group of about ten of his friends were standing near a little heating oil tank that used to stand near the church, close to a light on the corner of the church. "Suddenly I got this weird feeling," he remembers. "I turned around and saw a man standing behind me." Kirkpatrick said he saw him clearly. "The man was stoic. He had parted hair, and a handlebar-type moustache, but not that long." He says he turned around, not freaked out for some reason, and told his friend, Amanda, who was standing near him, "Hey, Amanda. There's a man standing behind me."

No one else saw it, but Amanda and the others freaked out. About that same time another odd thing happened. Many of the group were smokers, but no one smoked at the cemetery. "I, Canaan, and Amanda—and maybe some of the others. saw a pillar of what looked like cigarette smoke—but wasn't. It then began moving toward the light on the church. Once it reached the light, the pillar of white smoke disappeared."

Everyone raced out of the cemetery. In the process, Amanda's shoes fell off; one on one side of the road, the other shoe on the other side. When they returned a short time later, both shoes were together, laces neatly tied, facing the road. That was weird, but it gets weirder.

The group returned to Kirkpatrick's home in two cars. He didn't describe the man he saw at the cemetery to anyone. One group went upstairs to talk about what they had seen, the other stayed downstairs. Later, Kirkpatrick's friend, Matt, described in exact detail the same man Kirkpatrick saw standing behind him.

A Household Haunt

Kirkpatrick's home is believed to be haunted by a former owner named "Randy," who was killed on George Road in a motorcycle accident.

Randy died in the same place on the same road as Kirkpatrick's good friend, Chucky.

He remembers one time being in bed in his bedroom, the same bedroom that Randy's son, Andy, used to have. "I looked toward the foot of my bed and a green apparition was standing there. I was only about eight or nine at the time; I pulled the covers over my head."

Another bedroom had more space, so Kirkpatrick moved into that one and left Randy's son's room. Today, he can sometimes hear Randy walk upstairs and down the hall to his old room. Randy will stop for a few seconds, then turn around and walk back downstairs. "It's almost as if Randy is still checking on his son, Andy, to see if he's okay." Kirkpatrick's father took his old bedroom and told Andrew he still hears the ghostly footsteps outside his bedroom door.

Another unusual occurrence that may be attributed to Randy, or perhaps a different ghost, is a particular sound that happens at a certain time of the night. Kirkpatrick says there's a porcelain mug downstairs. His mother keeps several items in it such as fingernail files and clippers, but the fingernail clippers have been missing for a while. At that certain time each night, he can hear the sound of a fingernail clippers being dropped into the mug. Yet, the fingernail clippers are still missing when the mug is checked. "The sound occurs a few moments after I shut off my nightstand light and lie down for the night," Kirkpatrick says.

Unnerving as these experiences might be to anyone else, Kirkpatrick says he's never felt anything "bad" about having Randy around. That doesn't mean he isn't occasionally unnerved, though.

Sometimes when he's at the computer at two or three in the morning, the hair on his neck will suddenly stand on end, as if someone is there with him. Something about that feeling prompts him to turn on all the lights. One day, instead of turning on all the lights, he turned around and said, "Hello, Randy. How are you tonight?" The "tension" immediately dissipated. Kirkpatrick says that by acknowledging Randy's presence, he may have formed a bond. He thinks Randy is good with their "relationship."

When Kirkpatrick's father took Randy's son, Andy's old room, he also heard ghostly footsteps, but sometimes he witness something; he'd see his bed depress. At first he thought it was their cat, Mittens. Kirkpatrick describes the cat as "twenty pounds of Garfield." Kirkpatrick's father would physically see the foot of the bed depress as if something heavy was on it, only there was nothing there. A minute later, the depression in the bed would disappear.

Randy isn't the only presence Kirkpatrick has felt in the house. Sometimes at night when he's in bed, his ears begin ringing. The ringing will get so loud that he can't physically move. "When I finally can move, I'd shake so hard, I'd physically move the bed," he says. He began to notice his ears would ring only when he was facing the wall with his back to the door. He's not sure why this happens, but when it does, he feels a presence. Now he tries to face the door when he's in bed.

He remembers one time in particular. When his ears started ringing, he felt a "body" get into bed with him. Though there was no one there, the bed depressed under the weight of the invisible trespasser. He then felt a body against him and arms wrap around his torso. Kirkpatrick said he couldn't take it anymore. He started yelling and cursing at whatever it was that was holding him to get off him. Suddenly, the invisible being next to him left. "I spent the rest of the night chugging Mountain Dew with the TV and all the lights in the house on," he says.

Alexander Middle School

In addition to the cemetery near Pittsville, Kirkpatrick has also checked out a number of other alleged haunted hotspots. An old girlfriend's father bought the old Alexander Middle School in Nekoosa, and he and their friends pretty much had access to the building whenever they wanted. At that time, desks were in the building as well as frogs in bottles of formaldehyde.

The owner's son, Bernie, along with Kirkpatrick and his old girlfriend, would walk around the big building. They would smell cigar smoke on the third floor, though no one was in the area. The night janitor at the school was said to smoke cigars.

When they went exploring, the trio always had the feeling that there was someone right behind them. Sometimes they would set up a projector in the library to watch a movie. Kirkpatrick says it's a strange room with steps in the middle and doors on each side of the steps, with a stage in front of the steps. They took a photo inside the library once that revealed oodles of orbs. He says, "The photo showed the back of the room opposite of the stage and up the stairs. A large orb was located in the upper right corner of the room above an old fire escape leading to the outside of the building. There were also dozens of small orbs scattered about the room in the photo."

Kirkpatrick says the building is also said to have an emergency tunnel that runs from the school to the paper mill, but they never found it while they were exploring.

Railroad Tracks

The railroad tracks off 72nd Street on the outskirts of Wisconsin Rapids is also said to be haunted. The story involves a mother and her sons at the turn of the century who went to the area to have a picnic. The boys, however, decided to play a trick on their mother and hid on her. They hid so well and for so long that she believed someone had kidnapped them. Distraught, she heard a train coming and threw herself in front of the train. The two young boys are said to have jumped out of some nearby bushes to surprise their mother just as she jumped into the train. Terrified they went after their mother jumping into the train themselves and being killed. Kirkpatrick says, "I have never heard anything audible at the tracks nor have I heard that that is the case, rather it is that orbs are reported visible moving about the tracks."

Now, during the month of June or July, when the accident happened, others say they have heard the train whistle, and the scream of the mother.

Kirkpatrick has been to the site a couple of times. Once he kept feeling that someone was tugging his sweatshirt. A friend that was with him claimed he was doing it, but Kirkpatrick says his friend wasn't close enough to touch him. Finally, the group started back to their car and call it a night, but then decided to walk down the tracks the other way, toward Wisconsin Rapids instead.

Alongside the tracks are woods. As the group walked, they heard something in the brush move along with them. The second they stopped walking, the noise in the brush stopped. This happened several times. Kirkpatrick thought it must be a raccoon or something. He flicked on his flashlight, thinking he'd see a pair of reflective eyes in the brush. Suddenly a horrible growling, snarling sound emanated from within the woods at the location that he shone the light. The group started running and the sound of something running parallel to them—on two legs—stayed even with them. None of them could see what it was. They couldn't take anymore and bolted. Kirkpatrick hasn't been back to the tracks since.

Suicide Cemetery

Kirkpatrick and his friends have also spent more than one occasion at Suicide Cemetery. No, the name of this cemetery isn't really Suicide Cemetery, it's Green Hill Cemetery, but Kirkpatrick and his friends call it that because of the number of suicide victims buried there. This little cemetery is located just off Highway Z between Nekoosa and the unincorporated town of Rome.

Kirkpatrick and his friends went there one evening, and he sat down near a tree by himself; he just wanted to sit somewhere quiet, as everyone else was rather loud. He didn't think much about what would happen with all the noise and commotion. Once he was settled, he watched a very light breeze swing the day lanterns (during the day they store a charge and at night the lights shine from the stored solar energy). Suddenly, a very strong gust of really cold air rose up behind him.

One of his friends, Steve, shouted that they were leaving with or without him. Kirkpatrick couldn't fathom what was going on. Steve asked, 'Didn't you see it?' Kirkpatrick said he didn't see anything. Steve told him that when they looked over at him because they heard the wind, they saw a pair of red glowing eyes about six feet off the ground race straight at his back and then disappear suddenly.

On a previous visit, a little girl ghost made her presence known by running between the graves. Kirkpatrick still isn't sure what the pair of glowing red eyes were. Maybe he's better off not knowing...

A Chuckling Spirit

Not all the spirits or ghosts in Kirkpatrick's life are strangers. A clairvoyant once told him she saw a man behind him that was chuckling. The man behind him told the clairvoyant that he had Kirkpatrick's back. She asked if Kirkpatrick knew who the man was.

Kirkpatrick told her to describe the man. She said the spirit was really tall, slouched, kind of hunched over with a scruffy beard and an odd smile. She said, 'He chuckles a lot. Does that make sense?'

It made perfect sense. Kirkpatrick lost a very good friend to a motorcycle accident that he'd witnessed. He always blamed himself for not being able to do more. Kirkpatrick even got a tattoo with Chuck's name and date of birth and death. He's glad to know that his old friend, Chucky, has his back.

Though Kirkpatrick is busy with school, a job, and life in general, he hasn't ruled out more ghost hunts in the future.

Oakfield Apartments

Two female apartment dwellers in these 28th Street apartment buildings have had ghostly experiences here. The first is a young woman in her twenties who lives on the second floor of one building. The ghost that shares her apartment is not friendly.

Several times she's been in her bedroom or bathroom when things begin leaping off shelves. She's raced back in the room only to see more things leap off.

In addition, she's heard whispering in her ear and felt someone brush past her with a cool breeze. These things might be unnerving, but she says it gets worse. She's seen a ghostly face staring at her from her second-story deck that disappears the second she screams.

The other apartment dweller, a middle-aged woman, lives on the first floor in a different building. Her experiences include a picture that continually moves in the opposite direction it was hung, a tray that shot off the top of her television, and the sound of someone clearing their throat right next to her.

The buildings aren't that old. The two women have no clue who could be haunting either of their apartments.

Old Irving School

Located near the corner of Apricot and 12th Street, this old brick school is no longer in use. Many paranormal groups and just groups of teenagers come here hoping to witness paranormal activity firsthand, but this was before it was sold to a private party.

Old Irving School, Wisconsin Rapids.

Joe Bachman, of Wisconsin Rapids and a former resident of Las Vegas, lived here for about a year before learning about the old abandoned school. He went with a couple of his friends to see if the old school lived up to its reputation of being haunted. "The doors are chained up, it looks run down and desolate, and I gave it a shot one night with a few of my friends," he says. "Mind you, I was with a group of women who did not take the prospect of ghostly activity lightly, and preferred to stay in the car, so I investigated myself. With the doors locked and no way inside, the best I could do was cup my hands around my eyes and peer into the window.

"To my surprise, I witnessed a faint blue light in the distance. I looked behind me and realized that this was not a reflection of any kind and I looked back and watched the light fade away. Just that second, suddenly, something tapped the window from the inside. Well, needless to say, I jumped with surprise and I think the girls in the car noticed as well. I could see plainly inside and I know I saw nothing that could cause such tapping. By this time the women in the car were yelling at me to get back and I did. There is something weird about that school."

Another amateur investigator says he remembers going there and experiencing the same thing. He was pushed out of a window he was trying to climb into.

The impressive bell that used to be on the tower is now on the ground. An entrepreneur is said to have plans to renovate the school and turn it into a nice bed and breakfast or an apartment building. This wouldn't surprise me. The old Irving School is in a well-kept neighborhood.

3

Southern Wisconsin Ghosts

City 98: Ashippun

Abandoned Ashippun School

This school itself is said to be haunted in some stories. Others insist it's the playground that is haunted. The school, no longer open, it located north of Ashippun of County O.

Some say just a drive-by is enough to give them the creeps. Ghostly children have been seen on the school grounds and near the road.

A former female teacher's illuminated ghost was also said to have been spotted in a window.

City 99: Bristol

Whispering Oaks Restaurant

Southeast of Burlington and not very far from the Illinois border is a restaurant with a haunting reputation. Located at 4410 200th Avenue, this eatery showed its first signs of paranormal activity when the owner bought the restaurant and began renovations. The owner's friends, who had come to help, took one look at the place, told the owner it was haunted and left.

A small child is one ghost said to haunt the Oaks. Many children who have come to eat there with their parents ask to play with this child. When the adults look to see where the child is pointing, there's no one there. One employee heard a child ask if he would play with them only to turn around and see no one.

Child's play is not the only activity going on here: A metal bucket launched itself from a shelf and narrowly missed an employee. Pans have left their hooks and arranged themselves in the shape of a fan on the floor. Tools disappear only to reappear elsewhere. Oh, and wine bottles in the storage area once began uncorking one after another. Cheers!

Come hungry, leave haunted—and happy.

City 100: Burlington

Coach's Sports Bar & Grill

Mary Sutherland, owner of Sci-Fi Café and Earth Mysteries Museum in Burlington has done an investigation of this bar and its ghost. Coach's is located in very haunted downtown Burlington.

She says, "While doing some photo shots of Coach's for the Haunted Burlington Ghost Walk, I managed to catch the infamous 'ghost' on film! At first I thought it may have been a water heater with something thrown over it...or a play with the shadows." It wasn't. She says that after she uploaded the photo on camera and saw the ghost on film, she immediately returned to Coach's. "I checked out every angle to see if it may have been the result of lighting. I also checked to see if there was a hot water heater there...something that would obstruct the view of the wall. As I stood looking down the hall located in the basement of Coach's, I saw nothing that would project the image of the ghostly apparition. As a matter of fact, as I stood looking down the hall, the wall was completely in view with nothing in front of it...unlike what the photo showed." There are three tunnel entrances in the basement of Coach's and all three are sealed. Sutherland wonders, "Are they sealed to keep people from going in...or are they sealed to keep 'something' from getting out?" One door is sealed with "center" bricks. Sutherland says, "All we know for sure about the tunnels is that they lead under the road. I have heard that they may have an entrance or exit of this tunnel at the old high school. I have yet to check that out. We also know that wherever there is a tunnel entrance, we have high paranormal activity."

Sutherland says patrons of Coach's, while coming out of the stalls in the restroom, which is in the basement, witnessed a large vanity mirror fly off the wall and hurl toward them. Just as it was about to hit them, it instantly dropped to the floor and smashed into bits and pieces. Photos that Sutherland took during her investigation show swirling energy and blurring. However, wherever there were lights, there were no signs of blurring. Sutherland says, "Wherever there are vortexes, spirit energies can manifest."

Coach's Sports Bar & Grill is located at 488 Milwaukee Avenue. Learn more about Mary Sutherland's Burlington Vortex Tours and Burlington Vortex Conference and Fun Days in the Attractions section of this book.

Dead Man's Hill

The old earthen mound known as Dead Man's Hill to the locals, is home to an old cemetery that is now used as a pasture. Cattle have knocked over many of the very old stones.

Like most of Burlington, the natives below the surface of the earth are restless. Ghosts have been spotted here—that is, ghosts you can see and those you can sense. While some say these spirits are Native American, some believe they are the souls of those buried in this old cemetery.

City 101: Cedarburg

Founders Cemetery Park

This cemetery is also called Founders Park or First Trinity Lutheran Church Cemetery; it was established in 1834, and the last burial took place in 1869. It's known for its stone monument that lists the names of the people buried here. Not surprisingly, many are early Cedarburg pioneers. If you're into cool, old headstones, you might want to reconsider visiting this cemetery. The original headstones have seen better days.

Some say they experience a range of feelings from unease to being enveloped in cold air. Like many other haunted hotspots, there are places in the cemetery where the hair on the back of your neck stands on end even when it's sunny and warm.

Many say this cemetery radiates negative feelings that make them feel uneasy and "upset." Some say they can't shake the feeling that they are being followed.

Founders Park was built as a memorial to the city's founding families and is located on Evergreen Boulevard.

Kuhefuss House Museum

This 1849 German-American homestead housed five generations of the Kuhefuss family until schoolteacher Marie Kuhefuss bequeathed the building to the Cultural Center in 1989. Despite the fact that this two-room structure is open for tours, the ghost there seems perfectly fine with sharing his or her residence. Visitors often experience the feeling they are not alone, even when they are.

The ghost said to haunt the building manifests itself as a cold breeze and a tickle in your ear, as if it is trying to speak to you. Some believe the ghost or ghosts could be Edward and/or Johanna Blank, who purchased the building in 1849, or later members of the Kuhefuss family.

The Kuhefuss House Museum is located at 1849 W63 N627 Washington Avenue.

Lincoln Building

This 1920s restored school room is just down the road from the Kuhefuss House Museum, and it is said to be just as haunted.

The building was also once Cedarburg's only grade school. Groups of children often tour this room. Some come away with more than an old time view of the past—some say they've seen shadows or ghostly children. This isn't a frightening event—the children just look like old time, very well behaved children.

City 102: Coon Valley

DiSciascio's Coon Creek Inn

DiSciascio's Coon Creek Inn, Coon Valley.

This Italian restaurant is located at 110 Central Avenue in a hilly, incredibly beautiful part of the state that calls to mind the mountainous regions of Europe.

Employees call the ghost in this very old two-story building, Mary. She's believed to have been a patron of the building when it was a bar.

Mary is said to be responsible for things flying off the shelves and cold spots reported in the restaurant. Many employees and patrons have reported seeing Mary.

In addition to serving exceptional Italian cuisine that has received rave ratings from food writers and critics, DiSciasio's also rents two cabins right next door to the restaurant. H & R Cabins come with a great view and modern amenities. No word if Mary stops by the cabins...but I wouldn't be surprised.

City 103: Cottage Grove

Church Street

The woods are alive! But some of this "aliveness" might be caused by things that are no longer alive.

The area said to be haunted is the wooded area on Church Street, which is located off Rinden Road. A ghostly cat is said to prowl the area where it was killed.

Another story features a man walking his dog: If you are walking and spot the man and dog ahead of you, then take a gander, the man and dog will be gone when you look ahead of you again. If you look behind you again, the ghostly duo will then appear there.

Other stories about the ghostly dog are borderline frightening. It's said if you chase the ghostly dog, it will reappear behind you and take you down by the neck.

Note: Don't chase ghost dogs. Just to be on the safe side.

Hope Cemetery

Pictures taken in this cemetery, less than ten miles from Madison, sometimes feature a little girl ghost. But that's not all: Random photos taken with different types of cameras show orbs and strange streaks of light near certain stones. EVPs taken in the cemetery also reveal voices that ask for help, and also voices that try to get you to leave.

The cemetery is located on West Cottage Grove Road, off County N.

City 104: Eagle

Rainbow Springs Golf Course

The golf course is located at Tuohy Road/ S103w33599 County Road LO. The ghost said to haunt the course and hotel is a previous owner who was in the process of building the golf course, but found himself short of money before it was to have been finished. His name: Francis Schroedel.

The Springs was built in the 1960s to be a grand hotel. It stood on a grand parcel: 900 acres off Highway LO. Schroedel poured millions of his own dollars into the hotel, but alas, it wasn't enough. Schroedel's friends have said the developer put a curse on his own hotel, by saying, "If I can't open it, no one will."

After Schroedel died, many different uses for the resort were suggested, including a casino, religious retreat, and retirement community, but none of these were ever realized.

One part of the 760-room hotel was used for years for the annual Haunted Hotel, but a fire in April of 2002 destroyed most of the 600,000 square-foot structure.

When it was the Haunted Hotel, visitors and employees alike remember feeling that they didn't want to be alone in the building. They also reported that it would get so cold you could see your breath and then the next minute it would be warm. The sound of someone walking upstairs could be heard by those below. A presence said to be Schroedel has also been felt on the well-manicured golf course.

City 105: Elkhorn

Peck's Station Road

As the name suggests, a locomotive station used to be here. Not anymore. There have been no trains, or even tracks for that matter, in the area for years. The station house is now a private house, yet you can sometimes hear the whistle of trains.

Many witnesses have heard the plaintive sound of a train whistle during the day and night when there is no train in the area. The only thing I heard was the sound of birds and insects. But I know a UW student from this area who has heard the train, so it must be a matter of timing, or maybe luck.

Want to try to witness the phenomenon yourself? Take Highway 12 north out of Elkhorn. Turn east on County ES. You'll see Peck's

Station Road about two miles down the road. It will be on your left.

City 106: Elm Grove

Sunset Playhouse

This Waukesha County theater opened its doors in 1960 and underwent numerous expansion in ensuing years. "Entertainment begins at sunset!" is its catchy catchphrase and seems to sum up its human and ghostly performances nicely and precisely.

Pinky, the ghostly actor said to haunt the theater can be heard backstage and also during performances. Doors open and close on their own and the sound of footsteps with no person attached are signs that Pinky may be close by.

Lester L. Schultz, known better by his nickname of Pinky, died in 1968 of a heart attack at the age of fifty-five as he left the stage after the first act. It was the poker game scene of "The Odd Couple" and he was playing mild-mannered Vinnie.

Schultz was a former Marine, salesman, and prominent actor who had been with the playhouse almost since it had opened in 1960. He is remembered as being a gentleman and a prankster. Once Pinky suddenly slammed the boardroom door shut on a group of people just to let them know he was there, too.

Visit the Sunset Playhouse at 800 North Elm Grove Road.

City 107: Ferryville

Swing Inn

This Crawford County establishment, owned by Janelle and Randy Peterson, is known for a ghostly presence with a very unusual name: Blue Moon. She was said to be a prostitute who was murdered long ago; no one caught the killer.

Long ago, Blue Moon and other ladies of "ill repute" used the Swing Inn as their base of operations. It was a very good location because railroad workers would jump off the train to indulge in liquor and women.

Though no one knows the particulars surrounding Blue Moon's death, many believed she met her end on the stairs. Many have felt cold drafts in this area and have heard the sound of footsteps on the stairs when business is slow.

Janelle says she awoke one night in the apartment above the bar to a very loud sound, like beer bottles tipping over. "Dang it! Somebody's down there!" she told Randy. An investigation the next day revealed nothing was broken or amiss.

Janelle says the previous owners, Kathy and Jerry, had many stories about the ghostly presence. She remembers one in particular. "One time Jerry bought Kathy flowers, six red roses and six yellow roses. But at the end of the night, there were six red roses and only five yellow roses. Kathy counted and counted, but one yellow rose had mysteriously disappeared. Kathy even called her sister to ask and her sister told her there had been six of each color."

Kathy and Jerry went home and when they returned to the Swing Inn the next day, there were six red roses and six yellow roses. Apparently, Blue Moon likes yellow roses.

Janelle told me that when she's in the kitchen, she often hears things making noise upstairs when there's no one there.

Janelle believes in ghosts and "likes having the ghost" at the inn. "She doesn't hurt anybody," she says. The Swing Inn is located at 106 Main Street. Stop by for a meal and a drink, and you just might be able to hear Blue Moon make her way up or down the stairs. "There's always something unexplainable going on," Janelle says.

City 108: Genoa

Londoner's Pub & Bistro

This restaurant, formerly Whisker's Old Tyme Inn, is located at 500 Main Street, not far from the western border of Wisconsin. It's now an English pub with an impressive beer list. No word on any ghostly sightings; you'll just have to stop by and ask. I hear the atmosphere and spirits are jolly good, though.

Before it was Londoner's, however, a former owner by the name of Kenneth Beck was said to haunt the building. Beck suffered a heart attack outside the inn, near a dumpster and died. Another former owner who lived upstairs, collapsed and later died, but not at the building. Beck was an avid fan of CNN. So much so, that when he was working, he would only allow that channel on the TV. When workers would walk out of the room with a certain channel on, they would sometimes return to find the station on CNN on the screen, even though no one liked that station.

That's not the extent of ghostly tampering, however. The lights, stereo, grill, television, and coffee maker would mysteriously turn themselves on. Dinner plates and glasses went missing. Footsteps could be heard making their way up or down the basement stairs.

A little bit of interesting trivia: A roller skating rink was once located upstairs. Yes, upstairs. Imagine the noise below! There was once an accident on the nearby Mississippi River; the rink was used as a makeshift morgue.

City 109: Hartland

The Hartland Inn

In the 1900s, Max Meier's Hartland Inn was a hotel and restaurant. Now, the downstairs of this four- star establishment is a restaurant.

Most of the recent paranormal activity said to occur in the building centers around a young girl dressed in Victorian-era dress—some say an early 1900s sailor outfit. This girl has been spotted in the basement.

Before that, several staff members reportedly heard "blood curdling" screams coming from that same area. A search of the area turned up nothing out of the ordinary.

I couldn't find anyone who was willing to admit to seeing or hearing a ghostly presence at the restaurant, but I did hear from plenty of people who raved about the food.

Max Meier's Hartland Inn is located at 110 Cottonwood Avenue.

City 110: Horicon

Tallman Home

This story is a classic Wisconsin haunting worth mentioning, even though the home in which the "evil" haunting took place (in 1986) is now said to be poltergeist-free.

The Tallman family was said to have had no trouble when they first moved into this nice ranch home. Then they bought bunk beds for the kids and placed the beds downstairs. The kids immediately got sick, so they moved the beds upstairs. From there, things in the home took a big turn for the worse.

The Tallmans' young son awoke one night to the sound of the radio playing on its own, and he could see the dial moving as though someone was touching it. You guessed it—no one was there. The radio was taken out of his room.

One time, Mr. Tallman placed a paintbrush on the table, only to return to find the paintbrush in the paint can, bristles facing up.

Another time, Tallman's daughter said she saw a "witch" with fire at her bedroom door one night. The Tallmans' son also saw an old woman at his bedroom door.

The most disturbing event took place one fateful morning near the end of the Tallmans' stay at their home. Mr. Tallman had just finished his night shift and returned home. He heard a voice outside, walked around the house to investigate and saw what he believed to be his garage on fire. He ran his lunch pail into the house, ran back out to the garage, but there was no fire. Undoubtedly unnerved, he walked into the house, realizing as he entered that the door was locked. At that moment his lunch pail flew in the air and a mist appeared. It spoke to him: "You're dead!"

The Tallman family soon moved out. As they drove away, they took one final look back at their home and saw red eyes looking back at them.

The infamous bunk beds were later destroyed, and burned.

The house is located on Larrabee Street, near the corner of Washington.

City III: Hubertus

Fox and Hounds Restaurant

Fox and Hounds Restaurant, Hubertus.

There's nothing about the outside of this restaurant (which is part of an original log hunting cabin) that would give you the idea it's haunted. The restaurant and landscaped area around it look modern and…okay, maybe hauntingly beautiful.

Ray Fox, a previous owner, is said to have remained at the restaurant after he died. Fox was a painter when he was alive; some of his paintings were on display at the time paranormal activity was said to have taken place in the building. A painting that was once near a fireplace shows hunting dogs with ghosts hidden in the picture.

A ghostly Ray Fox is said to have been spotted in the basement, and this is where a wall of cold may sometimes hit you. Many say they feel as if someone is watching them the whole time they are in the basement.

I came here before it was open for the day. If the food is even half as good as the impression I got of the outside, it must do fantastic business. (It was sold in 2006 and renovated.)

Fox and Hounds is located at 1298 Friess Road.

City 112: Kansasville

Bong State Recreation Area

This area is located at 26313 Burlington Road—we're talking very close to Burlington, so one might expect at least a little strangeness. According to many, the area is rife with it.

First of all, this area was once a former Air Force base. Before that, it was crisscrossed by Indian trails, home to the last remaining pioneer log cabin in Kenosha County, and a pioneer cemetery that was said to have existed at the now nonexistent intersection of County LM and 18th Avenue.

The haunting feeling you get at certain places is said to be due to one of three things: the disturbed cemetery, the former Native American burial mounds said to be in the area, or the underground tunnels below the many parts of the recreation area.

The remains in the pioneer cemetery were said to have been moved to cemeteries in Milwaukee and Silver Lake, but some remains are thought to have been left behind.

In places along Burlington Road and County LM, apparitions have been seen. Sometimes, these apparitions don't disappear immediately, they are said to stare at you as you stare at them for a *loooooong* time. Finally, they disappear.

Victims of the Chicago mob as well as victims of biker gangs, are also said to be buried on the grounds, adding to the intense feelings of anger and confusion in some areas.

157

While many orbs have been captured on park grounds, many other photos have been taken that show white shadows, green swirls, and blue lights that do not correspond to anything.

Today, may report alleged UFO interaction here as well as ghostly interaction. The sounds of someone chasing you that you can't see have been reported.

The park is huge; after dark, don't wander off alone.

City 113: Lake Geneva

Hunt Club Restaurant and Legends Tavern

The Hunt Club Restaurant, located at 555 Hunt Club Court, at the front of the Geneva National Golf Club, has the largest wine list in Wisconsin, heartland cuisine to die for, and, if you believe the stories, at least three ghosts.

The three-story building was originally built in 1915, and was once a tuberculosis sanitarium for patients sent there by a large Chicago business. One story associated with that time period: When one patient died, the dog that lived at the sanitarium howled inconsolably all night.

The building has since been renovated and dishes up fine food and spirits. Apparently both kinds of spirits—a local psychic says the ghost of an eleven year old still walks up and down the stairs. A different psychic says it's the ghost of a German woman who was a nurse at the building when it was a sanitarium. So which is it? A kid? A woman? Both? Luckily the building has plenty of room for ghosts.

Some of the ghostly occurrences that take place here are the sounds of hollow footsteps upstairs, window and doors creaking open when they've been shut, and light switches that have a mind of their own. Some have even claimed to hear the empty howl of a dog—the dog that lived here decades ago when the building was a tuberculosis sanitarium, perhaps?

City 114: Pleasant Prairie

Pauper's Cemetery

This cemetery, located on Hwy H across from the police station, might need a little policing of its ghostly inhabitants. Moans and groans are common noises that come from the cemetery. Sometimes apparitions are seen. Sometimes they're misty; sometimes they're clear as life...

What's really creepy about this cemetery besides the fact that the residents of the cemetery didn't have a better place to be buried, is that the ground is literally giving way because of the wooden coffins the paupers were buried in. Yes, the coffins and all their contents are slowly becoming one with the earth.

Want to see for yourself? Start on Highway 50, then south onto County H. The cemetery is on the left side of the H, just a little bit south of County C. This cemetery is also known as Kenosha County Cemetery.

Spring Brook Cemetery

And another haunted cemetery in the little burg of Pleasant Prairie...

This one, located on Springbrook Road, also known as Highway 174, is known for its nice upkeep despite its small size, and the sightings of misty apparitions.

It was established in 1854, and has been giving cemetery-goers something to talk about, besides their dearly departed, for decades.

Balls of light have been seen among the gravestone. At night, some have seen blue light emanating from the oldest part of the cemetery.

City 115: Kenosha

Green Ridge Cemetery

This cemetery, combined with adjacent St. James Cemetery, is Kenosha's oldest and largest cemetery. It should not be surprising then, that many strange things have been seen and heard here.

First, you've got your ghosts; some are lifelike that disappear, some are misty shapes, and some are ghostly bodies that move between grave to grave in super-fast motion. Then there's the sound of full-bodied wailing and wailing caught on EVPs to go along with the sightings.

The main thing this cemetery is famous for is stone tossing. Yep, stone tossing. You throw a stone over the fence and you'll have the same stone or stones tossed back at you. I'm putting *that* on my to-try list.

The cemetery is located south of downtown Kenosha at the intersection of Sheridan Road and 66th Street.

Rhode Opera House

Most sites says the opera house opened in 1927. But the original Opera House was built in 1891 by Peter Rhode. Five years later, it burned down and was rebuilt in 1896. At the turn of the century, it began showing motion pictures.

For whatever reason, the building was demolished in 1926, and rebuilt in 1927. It was named The Gateway Theatre and had 1,250 seats. It operated that way until 1963 when it was renamed Lake Theatre, and closed in 1984.

The Lakeside Players took over the tenancy in 1988 with the name of the building reverting to "Rhode Opera House." This community theater group is still located there, and doing a fine job.

As far as ghosts go, many people have either heard or seen them in this historic building. These ghosts are actors who have performed here and are usually seen or heard backstage. A young man ghost is believed to sit in the rear of the auditorium during rehearsals. One member of the stage crew felt a presence just before a "cold, black cloud" passed through him.

Other memorable ghosts: a laughing ghost and a pleasant-smelling ghost who made her presence known by the women's washrooms. This ghost went one step further—she thanked guests for attending the show! A DJ ghost who died of a heart attack also makes his presence known by moving curtains.

City 116: Kohler

The American Club

The American Club, a five-star, Tudor-style hotel, which opened its door some ninety years ago, is included in the *Historic Hotels of America*. It's also said to be haunted.

The oldest part of the hotel, the east wing, is the part that is said to be the most haunted area of the beautiful old hotel. This is where a woman hung herself in Room 209. She is also said to stand near the fireplace in the Washington Room.

Another haunting associated with the hotel is that of the third floor. It is said a murder took place in one of the rooms on that floor and that a ghostly man can be seen walking down the hall away from that room. Lights in the east wing are also said to be manipulated by ghostly hands.

One witness saw a man wearing frumpy attire inside the hotel; this is something you wouldn't most likely see at this hotel. Nevertheless, the witness bid the man, "Good evening," and walked away from him. When the witness passed the man, he felt strange, turned around, and was stunned to find the man had disappeared. Just like that. The witness called security. When the tape of the exchange was reviewed, it showed the witness waving and talking to someone who wasn't there.

Witnesses have also recently reported seeing an older man in the back halls who disappears as you approach.

The American Club is located at 444 Highland Drive.

Riverbend Mansion

The magnificent mansion, also known as the Old Governor's Mansion, was built in the early 1920s and is located at 1161 Lower Road, near Lost Woods Park. It is located on the Sheboygan River, where there are many sharp bends, hence the name. Trees buffer the mansion from regular folk like you and me—so you'll need private membership if you want to see for yourself if the stories are true.

Today, Riverbend is used as a retreat for small business conferences, private entertaining, and other special gatherings. If humans can't resist the informal and formal gardens, tea-house, and self-piloted boat for river cruises, you can't expect ghosts to resist, can you?

Visitors have reported feeling cold spots in many places here as well as seeing ghostly mists.

The ghosts of Walter J. Kohler Jr., a former governor of Wisconsin, is thought to be responsible for the ghostly presences said to be felt here—especially after the last renovations.

City 117: Lake Delton

Ringling Road

Sightings of a ghostly woman have been seen at the road's edge. A shack just off the road is also said to be haunted by a man who hung himself.

I drove down most of this road and didn't see anything I would call a shack. I didn't see a ghostly woman, either, but residents of the area say this road is "eerie" at night and they don't like to walk it alone.

One group of teens I spoke to in town said they, "go to the road all the time." They've not only seen apparitions; they've seen a moving blue-white light that seems to be walking toward the road straight at them. One said when she returned home, she felt as if something "bad" had followed her.

Seth Peterson Cottage

This unique cottage, designed by Frank Lloyd Wright in 1958, is said to be haunted by a presence that manifests itself as cold spots and shadows. While no one is saying it's the ghost of Frank Lloyd Wright, they're not really saying who it could be it, either.

Residents of the Wisconsin Dells area say they've heard that a ghostly couple has been spotted in the area near the cottage. This couple is dressed in 1950s style and seems very lifelike until you try to approach them. Then—poof!—they're gone.

The cottage is located very near beautiful Mirror Lake State Park at E 9982 Fern Dell Road. It's not open for tours; if you want to check out the house for any reason, you'll have to check for the rare times it is open to the public.

City 118: Lake Geneva

Saint Killians

The graveyard is all that remains of this haunted area. The church was condemned years ago and was burned down by the Lake Geneva Fire Department for training purposes. Before the church was destroyed, there were reports of shadows that followed you, the sound of a bell ringing, and a motley assortment of other noises.

Some say devil worship is still going on in the area of the cemetery. If this is true, they're tough—the smells here are not for the faint-hearted or faint-nosed.

Many paranormal investigators come here to see if the strange sights, sounds, and smells are paranormal or just plain normal. It's no surprise that the verdict is both.

Dark shadows moving across the gravestones, and past visitors as they walk, have been reported, as well as strange mists that swirl around the stones and through the graveyard. Odd smells that have been noted in the graveyard seem to have a very normal origin: There's a swamp near the cemetery—a very stinky swamp.

City 119: Madison

Sanitarium

The current Northport Office of the Dane County Department of Human Services was once the Lake View Tuberculosis Sanatorium. Ghost hunters call it the sanitarium now, although the correct spelling should be "sanatorium" to follow the original spelling of Lake View Tuberculosis Sanatorium.

It's quite easy to find. Located on 1202 Northport Drive/Hwy. 113, it literally seems to jump into your line of vision, no matter what lane of traffic you're in, from its monstrous perch at the top of the hill. It's the veritable definition of the word *imposing*. In front of the building on a clear day, you see downtown Madison.

In the winter, people sled down the huge hill, many unaware of the haunted woods above them.

The sanitarium (especially the woods and cemetery at the top of the hill) is at the top of the investigative wish list of professional investigative teams and amateurs alike. Some say the ghosts there are the result of the many that undoubtedly lost their lives at the sanitarium; others believe the place is haunted because of its location on a hill overlooking water; this is said to indicate that the spirits here are Native American.

One thing that makes this site so unusual is the number of people who believe the ghosts of the sanitarium chased or forced them out. Worse—many believe the evil spirits of the sanitarium followed them home.

The first story comes from a woman who can "feel" the presences of spirits. She's visited the sanitarium a half dozen times and plans more trips in the future. She says she believes the building itself is not haunted, but says it gives off a strong psychic vibration. She believes the buildings around the sanitarium that have been called haunted by many, are like the sanitarium—not haunted.

However, she believes the cemetery and woods exhibit definite signs of psychic activity which include cold drafts that envelop you, mists that show up on film that are not there when you look at the cemetery or grounds in person, and also the sound of voices.

These voices are disturbing because, though they are low in volume, they send a chill through you. "The eastern end of the cemetery that borders the woods is the best place to experience this negative psychic energy," she says.

She believes the woods themselves are haunted by an angry presence. "Or evil," she says. Though she hasn't seen a ghost herself, others she's talked to have seen ghosts here. She thinks one explanation for the ghosts is the two outbuildings in the area which are now only foundations with smoke stacks. These ghosts might have spent time there in life, or passed away there. It's also rumored that the dead from the sanitarium were burned in the smoke stacks. It's also believed the nurses' barracks, one of these buildings, was connected by an underground tunnel to the main building.

"The evil presence in the woods could have another explanation," she says. "I believe there is a good deal of satanic goings-on there. I've seen bones and clumps of hair on the ground that seemed to be in some sort of pattern."

Lots college kids go to the woods and cemetery to check out the site. "Be very careful if you decide to visit the woods and cemetery," she says. "Come prepared for what you might encounter, human and otherwise."

The spirit's might linger with you longer than you would like.

"I'm probably the most skeptical person you ever met," Krystal M. says by way of introduction. "But I know what I felt and saw. It scared me so much, I'll never ever go back to that place." *That place* is the sanitarium.

Krystal moved to the area a year ago. She says she didn't believe in ghosts, but she didn't *not* believe in ghosts, either. Her cousin told her about the sanitarium and all the things that had happened to her when she'd been there. Her interest piqued, Krystal agreed to go with her cousin to visit the sanitarium woods.

They parked near the sanitarium a little before midnight. Krystal thought the idea of going there at midnight was a little hokey, but she's a black belt and felt certain she could take care of herself and her cousin should their plans go awry.

"We were just past the water tower, when my cousin—at least that's what I thought at the time—pulled my ponytail so hard, it actually yanked my head backward. I lost my balance and fell down. I immediately started yelling at my cousin, which in retrospect was kind of stupid. She was a good yard in front of me. She couldn't have yanked my hair."

Krystal admits it freaked her out. She spun around but didn't see anything, even when she moved her flashlight all around her. As she turned to look at her cousin, she felt someone tap her on the shoulder—hard.

"My cousin must have seen the look on my face because she asked me what was wrong. I told her someone tapped me on the shoulder, expecting her to say 'I told you so,' or something like that. Instead, her eyes got really big and she started running away from me."

This is where you or I might have turned tail and raced back to the car, but not Krystal. "That's when I got mad. I thought she was playing a trick on me, but then again, she looked really scared. I remember thinking it was impossible for anyone to manufacture such a genuine look of fear."

Krystal turned around and found herself face to face with...well, she's still not quite sure. "It was human-sized, but like a gray mist in the darkness. And it was really close to me. The next thing I knew, it slapped me on the side of my face. The weird thing is it really hurt." That's where all her martial arts training went out the window. "I turned around and ran after my cousin, screaming my head off."

164

She remembers that the air seemed to go really cold then, too. She also noticed a "stink" in the air that hadn't been there when they'd arrived. She says she still marvels that she could put one foot in front of the other because she was shaking so hard.

Krystal says she and her cousin stopped short in the cemetery. It was very quiet. She doesn't remember any kind of noise whatsoever. And just like that, a light rose from above a grave. It wasn't white or yellow like a flashlight might make, it was more of an orange-red color.

Neither of the women could move—or breathe. They watched the light head straight for them and then disappear into thin air. That might have been comforting, but for Krystal, that was it. She'd heard and seen and felt more than she ever dreamed possible. She wanted to get away from the sanitarium, and fast.

Her cousin was quick to agree. They grabbed each other's hand and started back to the road. Neither of them said a word, but someone or something was still nearby. They kept hearing harsh whispering in their ears. They looked at each other, burst into tears, and started running back to the car.

But that wasn't the end of the story. Sitting in the locked car, sobbing and shaking, they heard the low sound of whispering again. They both looked at each other, frowned and looked out the car window.

On the side of the car closest to the woods, was that same blob of gray mist that had "slapped" Krystal when they were near the cemetery.

"I started screaming at my cousin to get us out of there. I stayed at her house for the rest of the week. I still get nightmares about the mist and I swear sometimes I still hear that horrible whispering in my ear."

When I ask her if she thinks the ghostly presence that assaulted her at the sanitarium is still with her, an angry look flits across her face. "I pray to God that it went back to the sanitarium where it belongs. I didn't do anything to it, so why would it still be here with me?"

Scotty Rorek, co-host of Spooks R Us (see Attractions section) recently gave me a day tour of the area. He and other members of his group, Madison Researchers Into the Paranormal, have investigated the area numerous times. They all agree it's an intriguing place. While doing research on the history of the site, one ruined foundation was identified as having once been part of a pig barn.

The woods to the side of the sanitarium are huge, and it's a beautiful place to take a walk, even if you aren't in the mood to seek out paranormal beings. Other buildings besides the main building are not open to the public, but a peek inside makes one instantly wonder if ghosts reside here, too, even if humans no longer do.

The outside corner of the main building is said to be a place where many get the feeling they're being watched, and just plain strange feelings. No matter what you experience here, one visit won't be enough.

Williamson Street Pub and Grill

This pub and grill on Williamson Street is said to have a whistling ghost in residence. Employees of this popular eatery say they've heard very loud whistling in their ears when no one was nearby. Inanimate objects have sometimes taken on a life of their own and leaped off shelves or raced along the floor.

Patrons have also said they've felt tapping on their shoulder when no one was close enough to have tapped them.

The sound of a baby crying and also a woman laughing have been heard in the bar when only two people were present—both men.

City 120: Menomonee Falls

Grace Evangelical Lutheran Elementary School

This is like many other elementary schools in that children sit at desks. Unlike other schools, sometimes the children are said to be ghosts.

Located at N87W16171 Kenwood Boulevard in Menomonee Falls, this school is attached to the church. No one knows why ghost kids are said to sometimes attend the school; no children are known to have died here.

Another strange presence is located in the area of the stage. Odd noises such as things dropping when they haven't actually dropped, and the sound of whispering in empty rooms have been reported.

The church borders a city park to the south and is situated in a nice residential area.

Main Street

This major road runs through the middle of Menomonee Falls. It is believed that the road itself is haunted by a man who was run over and killed when the town was first settled.

This man has been witnessed walking down the sidewalks along Main Street and also in the hallways of North Junior High, just a couple blocks from Main Street.

One Menomonee Falls resident told me it's just a ghost *story*, but admitted he has heard the same story about a tall man in old-fashioned clothing walking down Main Street during the day and night.

Those who have spotted this ghostly man say he appears to be talking to himself as he walks. Some say he appears very real; others say he is more of a shadow man.

This ghost has turned into somewhat of a scapegoat. He's been blamed for a number of burglaries and arsons in town.

City 121 Milwaukee

Ardor Pub & Grill

Surprise! One of the most famous and deadly fires in Wisconsin's history took place on the very site of the building that houses this restaurant. The Newhall House burned down in 1883 and more than seventy people lost their lives in the fire.

After the fire, some say ghosts could be seen walking from the rubble as if nothing had happened.

Today, waitresses say they hear noises that defy explanation. Some have reported seeing streaks of light. I spoke to one customer who says he didn't know the history of the place, stopped in for a bite, and felt someone tap him on his shoulder. As he turned around, the hair on his

Ardor Pub & Grill, downtown Milwaukee.

167

neck rose. He turned to find no one there. He also said an extreme blast of cold enveloped him. It was like opening the door of very warm house in the middle of January.

Guse's City Hall Pub & Grill

It's no longer in business for the living, but there's a very good probability that the ghosts that reside at 1009 North Old World Third Street haven't noticed.

When the building was open for business, a man and a woman from an era long gone were seen dressed in 1800s garb floating through walls. This same pair was seen by guests of Guse's, reflected in mirrors. The ghostly guests are believed to be former patrons.

It will be interesting to see if the ghosts like the next business that occupies the building enough to make themselves known.

House of Frank N Stein

How can you not love the name of this wiener bar? This building was once a funeral home, as can be seen by its telltale architecture. When Leszynski Funeral Parlor left the premises to make way for House of Frank N Stein, the interior didn't undergo much of a change.

House of Frank N Stein, Milwaukee.

The dish room is said to haunted. Patrons, when in this room, say they are enveloped by cold drafts and disturbingly odd feelings. Could it be because this establishment was once a funeral home, and some of the odd feelings may be caused by the dead people who may still be lingering here?

House of Frank N Stein is located at 726 East Center Street in the heart of Riverwest. It has recently been repainted and outfitted with new light fixtures. Here's hoping they will shed some light on the ghosts said to haunt this affordable, super cool eatery. When was the last time you ate at a former funeral parlor?

Landmark 1850 Inn

Haunted! That's what many people say when they hear the name of Milwaukee's oldest tavern located not far from Mitchell International Airport. If patrons of the two-story brick building haven't personally experienced seeing something "strange," someone they know most likely has.

A female apparition has been seen by numerous employees. The ghostly visitor was wearing Victorian-era attire as she walked down the back stairs. It's not hard to imagine such a sight from the outside of this beautiful stone building, or the inside. I've been told by one patron that he's seen a ghostly female face in the upper window of the parking lot side of the building and was told by staff that no one was upstairs.

Landmark 1850 Inn is located at 5905 S Howell Avenue.

Milwaukee School of Massage

Hearing footsteps and voices when no one is there can be unnerving, but what if you actually saw the ghost responsible for said activity? Students of this school have seen apparitions in their peripheral vision, but the owner, Wanda Beals, has actually seen the ghost said to haunt the building and has named her Julia. Julia is an elderly lady believed to have been the former owner of the building.

The building is located at 830 East Chambers Street in a nice residential area of Milwaukee.

Pabst Mansion

Beer baron Captain Frederick Pabst may haunt this incredible Flemish Renaissance Revival-style mansion built in 1892. The thirty-seven-room mansion, located at 2000 West Wisconsin Avenue is said to be unusually

Pabst Mansion, Milwaukee.

quiet when no one is taking a tour. During those times, footsteps can be heard on the third floor.

Captain Pabst died in 1904. His wife died two years later in 1906. Their heirs put the mansion up for sale, and in 1908, the Archdiocese of Milwaukee purchased the building. It was used as the residence of the Archbishop. No word on whether Pabst paid anyone a visit during that time.

In 1975, the Archdiocese put the mansion up for sale with the hopes that someone interested in preservation would buy it. Unfortunately, that didn't happen. It was sold to a party who was going to demolish it to make room for a parking structure. If Pabst knew of these plans, there was sure to have been a lot pacing going on in the third story of the mansion.

Luckily, fate intervened in the form of Wisconsin Heritages, Inc., at that time a fledgling preservation group. Lucky for us and Pabst too, the mansion is now safe and has been open to the public since May of 1978. In the same year, the Board of Directors renamed the organization designed to protect and maintain the organization "Captain Frederick Pabst Mansion, Inc." The good captain can relax and stop pacing now.

There are others who believe the haunter of the mansion is Mrs. Pabst, happy her home is still lovely and standing majestically in downtown.

Could be. Some say the footsteps are sometimes light, like those of a woman.

Experience the beauty of the mansion and maybe a Pabst ghost for yourself. It is open year round and will give you memories you will never forget.

The Rave/Eagles Ballroom

Ask anyone's who has attended a few concerts here if they've noticed something strange about the place, and chances are, they'll say they have.

This building, constructed in 1926 as a social club sponsored by the Eagles Organization, is now a venue for rock concerts. It is reportedly a haven for a menagerie of ghosts.

One of the strangest things you might notice is the smell of chlorine from a pool that no longer exists. A young man who died in the pool after suffering a heart attack is believed to be responsible for the lingering odor.

Performers, patrons, and employees have told many stories of disembodied voices and cold spots. Others have had the unnerving experience of feeling something pass through them when they are alone.

The building, located at 2401 West Wisconsin Avenue, has a number of seats, especially Rave Hall, that are said to be already occupied. Concert-goers have reported feeling that someone is sitting next to them, staring at them, when the seat is empty.

Another inexplicable sound is that of happy children playing and children that *aren't* so happy. This of course, occurs when no children are around.

Negative energy in the form of cold spots are said to materialize when you are in proximity of the ghost of the former men's shelter director.

I talked to a group of concert-goers who say they never wander anywhere alone; it's just too scary. One said he's heard the sound of shuffling feet behind him when he was alone.

While some people like to say one ghost in residence is that of Buddy Holly, most believe it is not. Holly's last gig actually took place here in 1959 in the Eagle's Ballroom. He died in a plane crash shortly after. Holly, in life, gave off different vibes than the ones given off by most of the ghosts that are said to reside here.

Shaker's Cigar Bar

This building, located at 422 South Second Street, was once a wooden barrel factory. It was built in 1894 and is believed by the owner, employees, and patrons, to be home to many ghosts because of the many different apparitions that have been seen.

In addition, cold spots can be felt throughout the building and poltergeist activity has also been observed on the lower level of the building.

A little girl ghost in 1800s dress is the ghost most often seen. She is said to frequent the ladies room.

City 122: Mukwonago

Heaven City Restaurant

This heavenly establishment has the best of both worlds: great food and at least one ghost. A woman has been seen floating on the premises. Items have also been observed flying across the room.

The ambience, food presentation, and service are said to be indeed heavenly. This was also a former hangout of Al Capone, and some believe he and/or some of his hangers-on are still hanging around. Psychics and regular customers agree the place exudes ghostly vibes.

To have an extraordinary dining experience (with a side of ghostly activity, perhaps) drive to S91 W27850 National Avenue.

Lower Phantom Lake

Sewall Andrews was the first white settler to this beautiful area located in Waukesha County. He arrived here in 1836 and built the first brick house (now a museum) in the area in 1842. Andrew's second wife, Jane, like many early settlers, was said to embrace the paranormal and even held séances. Strangely, she isn't one of the ghosts believed to haunt this lake. The ghosts said to haunt Lower Phantom Lake are Native American spirits.

Lower Phantom Lake was created when Upper Phantom Lake settlers built dams that caused flooding. The original lake was called Spirit Lake by Native Americans and had a ghost story attached to it.

The story involves a love triangle. Yes, love triangles happened even before movies and TV. It involved a beautiful Indian girl who was desired by a member of her own tribe and also by a member of another tribe that her own tribe didn't exactly like. Let the intrigue begin...

As sometimes happens, things went downhill from the start. The beautiful Indian girl's suitor from her tribe began wooing her while the suitor from the other tribe took a different route and began trying to win the Indian girl's father over. Waste of time, it turns out.

One September night, the two suitors dueled to the death on Spirit Lake. The winner: the ruler of the underwater kingdom. What?!

While the two young men were busy trying to kill each other in separate canoes, the young Indian girl was pulled, screaming, from her canoe and dragged beneath the surface of the waves.

Every September a reenactment of this event takes place. Every year, ghostly lights on the lake have been spotted as well as unearthly sounds. Every year, someone spots two ghostly men dueling in canoes and a hand reaching up to grab a ghostly maiden.

City 123: Oostburg

Veterans Park

A creek runs through this nice park located in Sheboygan County. The ghost in the park, which has houses on all four sides of it, is related to the small creek. A drifter was said to have drowned in it.

Not only has a ghostly man been spotted walking along the banks of the creek, the sound of moaning has been heard when no one was nearby. The man is said to walk into the creek and disappear if you walk toward him.

Strange noises have been noted in the sewer pipes, but this could be attributed to normal activity in the pipes.

One swing in the park has been observed slowly moving back and forth when there is no wind. In that same area, if you approach the swing to see what is going on, you will be "hit by a blast of cold air even if it's super hot outside."

Paranormal investigative teams have made trips here in the hopes of capturing paranormal evidence. I haven't found any that have so far, but it may just be bad timing. The ghostly man is said to reveal himself during the day and night.

City 124: Platteville

City Hall Park

This park is said to be haunted by ghosts from the 1800s. Men dressed in "mining type" clothing have been spotted walking through the park and ...right through trees.

A man leading a donkey has also been spotted in the North Bonson Street area. This man is wearing bagging pants, boots, and suspenders. The donkey wasn't wearing anything.

This may be a residual type haunting, as the ghosts seem to be performing tasks they did routinely in the past.

UW-Platteville

Delta Sig frat house is reportedly an old mortuary near the UW-Platteville campus. Many residents report seeing many apparitions inside and out of the frat house.

Unexplained sounds and objects that move on their own are said to be the norm at this frat house.

City 125: Plymouth

Yankee Hill Inn B & B

This inn is actually two separate buildings built by two wealthy brothers. One is referred to as the Gilbert Huson, the other the Henry Huson. Both were built in 1891. One is a Queen Anne style home, the other is an 1870 Gothic Italianate home. Both are on the National Register.

The buildings are located at 405 Collins Street, near the Kettle Moraine Recreation Area. This is one of the most beautiful places not only in Wisconsin, but the entire United States. One of the buildings—no one seems to be certain which one—is haunted. The building that is haunted features a third-floor ghost.

A mirror has reportedly shattered on its own, and footsteps are regularly heard in rooms that are empty.

City 126: Potosi

Brunner's Food Center

A miner was said to have been killed in the area of this store.

He can be seen walking away from the store, down the hill. No, he isn't carrying a bag of potato chips or a gallon of milk; he's carrying a pickaxe.

Brunner Food Center is located at 101 South Main Street, a hop, skip, and a jump from the Mississippi River.

Witnesses have been spotting miner ghosts in this area of Wisconsin for more than a hundred years. Oddly, they are usually walking somewhere; rarely if ever are they "mining."

City 127: Prairie Du Chien

Fort Crawford Cemetery

The fort was abandoned by the living in 1856, but the ghosts are still on duty in the 1829 Fort Crawford Military Cemetery. It's one of the U.S.'s smallest cemeteries with eighteen known internments and forty-six unknown. It was originally designed to be the final resting place of officers serving at Fort Crawford and their families.

The cemetery, located at 413 S. Beaumont Rd. is said to be a hotspot of paranormal activity, including camera malfunctions and severe unease at the site.

A related side story: The nearby hospital has been reconstructed on its original site and is now a museum. The room where Dr. William Beaumont performed digestive experiments is said to be a place where some experience strong feelings of unease.

Villa Louis

At first sight, you might wonder why this old house located at 521 N. Villa Louis Road, St. Feriole Island, Prairie du Chien, would be haunted. It looks, well…nice. Like many nice old places, a ghost of a long-dead ancestor is said to haunt it. But then again…maybe not.

This Victorian mansion on the corner of Villa and Bolvin is built on an Indian mound. Apparitions have been seen in the windows of the house and also on the grounds.

Wyalusing Academy

Many have seen a "wandering ghost" that vanishes into thin air in the area around the school at 601 South Beaumont Road. The ghost could be almost anyone. This site was once part of the second Fort Crawford. The first one was built on St. Feriole Island. John Lawler gave this site to Catholic nuns in 1870 to be used as a girl's school. It was then named St. Mary's Academy and educated young women for almost a century. St. Mary's closed in 1968. Now the Wyalusing Academy, a private institution, operates in the building. The school's mission is to help students who have had difficulty in traditional schools.

The ghost that haunts the building and grounds does not have difficulty making others aware of his or her existence. Students and nearby residents say they've also seen a bluish ghostly person peering out at them at night from darkened windows.

175

City 128: Racine

Elmwood Plaza

The back of the Eye on Video store, formerly Planet Video, is said to create feelings of extreme unease; more specifically, the doorway that leads to the office. This area is often cool when there is no reason. Doors close and movies jump off the shelves on their own. And no, not just the paranormal movies.

A shadowy figure has also been witnessed during early morning or late evening hours along the back wall of the store. A manager didn't know anything about the paranormal activity here, but when I called a different time, an employee told me the place is super creepy when she's alone and said she had to get off the phone.

The video store is located at 3701 Durand Avenue. Businesses around Eye on Video are also believed to be haunted.

Racine Country Club

The country club was said to have been a brothel in the 1920s and 1930s. The attic is the place believed to be filled with the spirits of prostitutes who were murdered in the building.

Shadows and cold spots are often noted by employees, past and present. The grounds aren't immune from ghostly influences, either. People have been seen on the course only to vanish into thin air, and these people weren't wielding golf clubs. The golf club is located very close to Graceland Cemetery; some say the ghostly shadows and people on the greens are restless residents of the cemetery.

The country club is located at 2801 Northwestern Avenue.

Winslow School

Over the years, the ghost sightings at and around this school have really piled up. One theory is because the school stands on the site of the city's first cemetery.

The building, erected in 1856 on top of the cemetery, is one of the three oldest school buildings in Racine. The bodies in the cemetery were removed by families before March 20, 1854, but did anyone make sure?

Apparitions, icy drafts, and general feelings of unease have been reported here. Winslow School is located at 1325 Park Avenue.

City 129: River Hills

Milwaukee Country Club

You're ready to swing when suddenly someone taps you on the shoulder. *Grrr*. Your concentration is ruined. You turn around, ready to give him or her a piece of your mind, but wait—there's no one there. Huh?

The ghost said to haunt the grounds may be a former member of the club just having a little fun. Or maybe trying to get even—in death?

Milwaukee Country Club is located at 8000 North Range Line Road.

City 130: Rochester

Chances Restaurant

Chances are good, if you spend any amount of time in this historic, old restaurant, you'll have a ghostly encounter. You see, Chances never lacks for customers, dead or alive. This restaurant, located at 205 West Main Street in Rochester, was formerly known as the Union Tavern.

In order to get a better idea of the ghosts that occupy Chances, it's important to know the type of clientele it served in its heyday.

Traffic on the United States Road became so heavy that, in 1848, a plank road was built. It was said that as many as 100 teams passed through town in the early morning hours, and it was not uncommon to see 40 or 50 wagon loads pass through town in a group.

Traffic on the plank road brought the need of lodging in Rochester. Two hotels were built, the Union House, and Meyer's Hotel. The Union House had a spring-supported dance floor on the second floor.

Levi Godfrey and John Wade built a double log house near the present site that was opened as the first tavern in western Racine County. Travelers between Racine and southwest Wisconsin stopped there to share meals or spend the night on the packed dirt floor.

Displeased Indians were said to have burned the tavern in the early 1840s. The property was bought by Peter Campbell, who built the existing brick building in 1843. He named it the Union House. Rochester was then the third largest city in Wisconsin and the Union House was one of the most popular stops cross-state. In 1856, a large stone addition expanded the Union House. A 2,000 square-foot dance hall took up most of the top floor; an expanded dining room was situated downstairs. The springboard dance floor, still intact, is believed to be among the last of its type in the state.

In the 1850s, railroads bypassed Rochester. The decline in business forced the Union House to close as a hotel. Prior to the Civil War, the Union House and the Willard House on the other side of the Fox River, reportedly hid slaves as part of the Underground Railroad. Legend has it slaves hid in the cellars of one of the other of these establishments until they could be sent on their way to their next stop. The Chances basement wall has an odd, circular hole in it that may well be an entrance to the old passageways.

In 1987, new owners bought the business because of its history. It looks pretty much today as it did a century ago, thanks to the well-preserved interior.

Employees first told the new owners about the so-called spirits that inhabit the building, but they didn't think too much of it. Soon, the owners noticed chairs pushed out from tables.

There may be as many as seven ghosts who haunt Chances. One is Sadie, a black woman and runaway slave who was a cook at the Union House. The other ghosts are known by descriptions. One is a woman who wears a green gown. Another is a woman who wears a blue dress.

Sadie was a cook who lived in the basement and only came upstairs when it was time to prepare meals. It's believed she doesn't have a good attitude toward the chefs that work at Chances; stove burners shut off when food is cooking. A door that leads from the kitchen to the basement does not stay shut, and food disappears. Maybe she's just hungry.

A Civil War soldier has been known to pinch female customers and wait staff. He looks so real that a cleaning lady quit—reportedly after seeing the ghost.

He pinches the ladies so much that everyone is pretty much used to it. The accompanying coldness is annoying, but at least you know who it is.

Legend also has it that the Civil War soldier asked his lady love, a ghost lady in a green dress, to marry him, but because she was a prostitute, she thought she was unworthy. She hung herself upstairs; he was said to have killed himself down stairs.

Stacy Kopchinski, co-owner of the restaurant with her father, Tom Schuerman, has also seen the face of a blond-haired woman staring out of an upstairs window as she's driven by late at night. A number of other people have asked who lives upstairs as they've seen someone looking out of a window, too.

I recently spoke to Stacy, who told me the restaurant continues to experience frequent paranormal incidents. In fact, so many have expressed in interest in the ghosts that reside at Chances, that she will be hosting her first annual Dinner with the Dead in October (see Attractions sections for more information) on the second story of the building. Up until now, this area was unused. Previously when Stacy would go up there, she got bad vibes. But since she's started preparing the area, she doesn't get any bad vibes. Maybe the ghostly residents are happy they'll be having company.

As far as recent ghostly occurrences—there are plenty. Stacy says when paranormal investigative groups come in, they always come away with something. She remembers one investigation in particular: "One group was upstairs filming in the dark. There were two of them and they were filming one end of the ballroom to the other. Suddenly they captured a white light that looked like a snake that was about two to three feet long. It seemed to wrap around one investigator before shooting into the wall," she says.

Are EVPs captured on the premises? You better believe it. "One group was asking questions, trying to get a response from the ghosts. There wasn't a peep during the entire session until the very end. That's when you could hear, 'Get the hell out!' and it was clear as can be."

Yikes! I don't know about you, but I want to know more!

Chances is located at 205 West Main Street in downtown Rochester.

City 131: Sauk County

Ghost Cows

Nothing says Wisconsin like a leisurely drive in the country and looking out your window to see cows placidly chewing their cud. Nothing says "What the—?" like driving through a herd of cows that disappear as you drive through them.

That's right. Ghost cows have been said to roam the roads of rural Sauk County since the 1950s. And these cows are memorable because they're Brown Swiss cows, not your usual garden variety black and white Holsteins you usually see in farm country.

So don't be alarmed if a small herd of Brown Swiss cows walk in front of your vehicle. Chances are pretty good they'll disappear if you hit them.

But just to be on the safe side, please brake.

City 132: Sheboygan

First Star Bank

A former janitor named Duke still calls this bank his home. He rattles doors around and is said to move things here and there.

The staff knows the sounds he makes and are not fearful of this very faithful employee who worked there until he died. Cold, unexplainable drafts are sometimes felt in some offices.

First Star Bank, now US Bank, is located downtown.

City 133: Sinipee

A Real Ghost Town

The entire of town of Sinipee is a ghost town in every sense of the word. It was once a thriving town, now no one lives there except ghosts. Lots of them, if you ask people who have been to the ruins of the town.

What's left of the town, now mostly farmland and countryside houses, is located three to four miles away from Dubuque, Iowa. The spring that fed the hotel is supposedly still there, along with the foundation.

The town was once the site of an incredible stone hotel, aptly named the Stone House. Two men who later became presidents—although one was a Confederate president—stayed at the hotel more than once.

Most reputable sources say the town was formed in 1838, though some say 1831. During the town's birth, more than twenty buildings were erected. In 1839, the town flooded, much like many Mississippi River towns of today. Back then, however, malaria spread from sitting pools of water. Almost all the good people of Sinipee died that year of the disease. By 1840, only two families remained in Sinipee and most of the almost-new buildings were moved to Mineral Point.

The ghosts of those who lived, worked, and played there in the 1830s are said to reveal themselves as voices heard on the wind and the soft sound of crying. Ghostly figures of children have been seen in grassy areas where houses once stood.

If you want to try to find the ruins of Sinipee, plan on spending some time there. Many who drive down for the day never discover the ruins of the hotel.

City 134: Slinger

Slinger Elementary and High School

Slinger High School has been deemed haunted for decades. It is believed that a student who was hit in the head by a shot put is responsible for the school's paranormal reputation. Other students who committed suicide or were killed in car accidents are also said to haunt the high school.

The locker room, gymnasium and nearby steps, and rooms near the gymnasium have been the scene of experiences that span the past two decades. The sound of racing footsteps has been heard in the gymnasium when it is black and deserted. Door and gates have flown open on their own. Even more frightening: When a door unexpectedly bursts open, it is inevitably followed by a blast of cold air. After you race away, recover from your fear and return, you find the door closed and no evidence that anything ghostly has occurred.

Don't think that students are the only ones who have witnessed impossible-to-explain events at the school, however. Janitors at the high school say they feel like they're being followed as they go about their daily activities and have also witnessed doors opening and closing by themselves.

Slinger Elementary School, which is next to the high school, is said to be as haunted as the high school though it looks very modern. Students at the school have seen a girl ghost walk through one restroom stall and walk straight out of the restroom.

The high school is located at 209 Polk Street. The elementary school is located at 203 Polk Street.

The town of Slinger may only have about 5,000 residents, but it knows how to party. The town holds an event called Spooky Slinger.

City 135: Stoughton

Investigation of Elsing's 2nd Hand Shop

by Paranormal Investigators of Milwaukee

Vicky Elsing of Elsing's 2nd Hand Shop and her husband, Phil, invited me to join a ghost hunt at their store on July 19, 2008. The Paranormal Investigators of Milwaukee (PIM) team was in charge of the overnight investigation.

Until that day, I had never met the Elsings. Vicky and Phil were not only gracious hosts, Vicky also provided gourmet handmade

Elsing's 2ⁿᵈ Hand Shop, Stoughton.

treats for everyone who stayed for the ghost hunt. I also met, Otis, the Elsing's dog, who is featured in my book, *Ghosts of Madison, Wisconsin.*

The ghosts have been so active that Vicky has written pages upon pages about the ghosts at the shop and has written a book about the paranormal goings-on titled, *Stoughton Wisconsin's The Grand Hotel Legacy: A story of ghosts and spirits within these walls.* You can also find Vicky's blogs about her experiences at: http://www.iamhaunted.com/ Vicky-E.

What makes Elsing so unique is her passion to understand the paranormal activity in her shop. She truly wants to know why the spirits in her shop linger and what they want. She admits to being frightened sometimes and confused by what the ghosts and ghost hunts at her shop reveal. But mostly she enjoys having them around.

PIM

I arrived at the shop a little early and took photos of the outside and met Vicky, Phil, and Otis. They invited me in to look around and then

Vicky and Phil left to take care of a few things before meeting back at the shop at 6 pm. At that time, I met members of the PIM team for the first time. Team members present for that night's investigation were founder Noah Leigh, Steve G., Candice K., and Karen K. All were professional and personable.

The group gathered baseline information including EMF, temperature, radiation, and humidity readings before we left the building to eat at the Koffee Kup. Also before we left, the sensitives, Candice and Karen, made a sweep of the building to gather their impressions. A voice recorder was left on while we were gone to pick up anything in our absence.

While Phil, Vicky, the PIM team, and I ate at the Koffee Cup, Noah talked to me about the group. Noah has been actively investigating the paranormal since October of 2006 and in February 2007, PIM was officially formed.

Noah says he and his group focus on the scientific aspects of investigation. Noah has a Masters degree in Epidemiology, and is pursuing a PhD in Microbiology and Molecular Genetics. To say science is a big part of his life is an understatement. Each member of the group does not specialize in only one area of investigation. This ensures that

Paranormal Investigators of Milwaukee (PIM). Pictured, left to right: Nick S., Karen K., Noah L., Steve G., Candice K., and Deidre J. Not pictured: Michael T. and Amy M. *Photo courtesy of PIM.*

if one member of the group cannot make it to an investigation, another member can easily take his or her place.

Some locations that PIM would love to investigate include Waverly Hills, Eastern State Penitentiary, St. Augustine Light House, and The Bird Cage, to name a few. They meet once a month to go over business, discuss upcoming investigations, and to go over evidence gathered from investigations they have already conducted. They also use this time to discuss possible investigations. Everyone in the group has the ability to bring an investigation to the group. One rule: The location must have publicly stated they are haunted, unless the person bringing up the investigation knows the owners of the location personally in some way.

When we returned to the building, Noah and the other members of the team once again went through the building, checking equipment and gathering impressions.

Vicky set out a veritable feast of gourmet popcorn and cookies for later (she should think about adding a café to her shop!) and Noah got the investigation underway after Phil and Otis, their dog, went home for the night.

The team discussed various aspects of the investigation. Noah paused and asked me if I had any questions after each new discussion. I learned at one point that a black ghost named Simon didn't want me there. I have to admit that this information unnerved me a little bit, but Noah assured me that this might even benefit the investigation.

Noah explained to me that if there was something that a spirit didn't like about me, the spirit might be more apt to try and communicate with the team in an effort to get me to leave, or to simply let it be known that the spirit was not happy with my being there. This would be helpful, as it would increase the probability that some sort of evidence could be captured. So even though I was a bit unnerved, I was excited to know that my presence might increase the possibility of success on this investigation.

The team tries to debunk odd occurrences by process of elimination. I learned that electromagnetic frequencies, or EMF readings are important because a decrease or increase in a baseline measurement can signify that an entity may be producing or using energy as it tries to manifest itself.

Noah told me a little about the EMF detectors PIM uses. "The detectors that our group uses are called Tri-field meters , a brand of EMF detector. They are special because they are 3-axis EMF detectors. This means they measure EMF levels on all three planes (XYZ: at once so you know that the EMF reading you are getting is the true reading.

If you use a single-axis meter, the reading you are getting may change if you change the orientation of the meter in space."

PIM also uses a pyrometer, which is a temperature device that samples the air temperature every one second. Noah says it's very sensitive and better for detecting cold spots than IR thermometers as the IR thermometer can only detect the temperature of a surface (and as far as he knows, entities don't have surfaces). "Plus," he says, "most IR thermometers only take readings every 15-30 seconds or so, so you could miss a cold spot in the time the device needs to take a reading."

The sensitives/psychics in the group, Candice and Karen, played a very important part in the evening's investigation. During the course of the evening, Candice made use of a pendulum and automatic writing skills. Karen and Candice also allowed me to hold the dowsing rods. This is one thing I was curious about. I wasn't sure if I believed they were a useful tool—or even if they worked at all. While they asked questions, I held the rods; they had no contact with them. The answers to their questions were revealed by the rods crossing and uncrossing in response to specific questions. At one point, not only was the hair on my neck and arms raised, so was the hair on my entire head! I plan on buying dowsing rods of my own and learning more about them.

While I spoke with Candice and Karen, Steve and Noah made sure cameras, etc. were set up the way they wanted. When we gathered as a group before lights went out in the shop, we heard from Candice, who said the shop was "way more active then the last time" they had been there. She told us about the presences that she felt there, including "Simon." Karen also told the group about her impressions. I made a mental note to never be alone in the dark building.

Noah and the team cut all power to the building at the breaker box in an attempt to remove all man-made EMF from the building. "This allows us to better control the EMF levels in the building so any anomalous readings we obtain during an investigation are more likely to be paranormal in nature and not caused by unshielded wiring or outlets," Noah explained to me.

Noah also used a digital camera that is sensitive to the IR wavelength of light. He said, "Though not a unique piece of equipment, I know of no other groups in the area that use it. It is interesting because we don't know what wavelength of light the entities may exist in, and as such we may be able to capture something shooting in the IR spectrum that we would not catch if shooting in the normal visible spectrum."

We shut off our phones, and Noah handed out UV flashlights to everyone. Noah told me: "I use UV flashlights because IR cameras are not supposed to be able to pick up the UV light. Now through testing, we find that when cameras are put into NightShot™ mode (the name Sony gave to its cameras that use IR light to shoot in the dark) all filters are removed and UV light is visible, although not as bright as we see it with our eyes. As such, we have fitted special filters to our cameras that will filter out the UV light. Why do we do this? Well if we are shooting video and we see a light anomaly and we were using regular flashlights with red filters (which many groups use) we would not be able to rule out that it wasn't one of our own flashlights that caused the anomaly (unless no one was in the building or something). By using the UV flashlights combined with the filters on the camera, we can be certain that any strange lights we see are not caused by us. This just allows us to control one more aspect of the investigation and prevents us from contaminating our own evidence."

The Investigation

One half of the group, Noah, Candice, and myself when to the attic, and Vicky, Karen, and Steve went down to the basement area of the shop. With the lights off, the evening took on an even more serious feel. Upstairs, Candice told Noah what she was seeing, and he, in turn, tried to get the ghosts or presences to react to his thoughts and questions. Among the presences Candice saw were two prostitutes. All the while, EVP equipment was running.

Vicky wrote down what happened to their group while they were in the basement: "We walked into the way back of the storage rooms, the room known as Simon's Room. We tried to make contact with him. Nothing seemed to be happening. We then headed into the furniture room. We sat down and did an EVP session. Karen also used a pendulum. I had never seen one of them work before, so that was very interesting. We asked questions and got answers. At one point the pendulum was swinging wildly. Karen had to ask it to please calm down. I really enjoyed watching all of this. We then went into the book room and did some more EVP and pendulum work."

Each group traded places later. "The next round, we all headed to the basement as a full team," Vicky wrote in her blog. "We all headed into the back rooms of the basement. We stood in different places and Candice said that the man ghost (Simon) was watching us. We all stood our posts to see if we could get anything to happen. Nothing happening, so we gave up and headed to the furniture room. We all spread out and started an EVP session. While doing this, Steve got a strange scent of roses. Candice also could smell the roses, but none of the rest of us could. Noah then found some bottles of perfume sitting behind Steve. One of the bottles did have the cover off. It must have been a customer checking it out and never put the cover back on. We then had Steve smell the bottle and he said it was not the same thing he was smelling. They then had Steve go to the far end of the room and I took the open bottle with me and sat it behind Steve. Steve then sat there and tried to see if he could smell the roses again. Nothing."

Vicky notes, "Now I would think if it was the perfume that Steve was smelling, then he would smell it on the other side of the room also, since I put the bottle right behind him. I then took a bunch of pictures and I got one picture with a moving bright orb in it."

"Candice then did what is called automatic writing. Noah would ask questions and Candice would write the answers on a paper. I had never seen that done before— it was all very interesting to me. I really enjoyed watching that. I cannot remember all the questions and answers. It will be written up in my report, though."

We all headed upstairs after this and talked as a group for a while. I left at about 2 am. Vicky went to bed a little after I left, and the PIM group slept downstairs in the furniture room.

Vicky says, "While laying in bed on the main floor, with no one moving around, I was almost asleep when I was startled by a sound. If I had dozed off, it sure woke me up fast. I can't really describe the noise I heard. It was almost like a screech. It was a very strange noise. I just thought to myself, maybe I was dreaming and I didn't really hear it. Then all of a sudden it happened again. The same noise. I have no idea what it might have been. That was the last of it. I then fell asleep and didn't wake until morning.

"After getting up in the morning, Steve came upstairs. He said after they went to bed, they all heard a very loud noise downstairs. They also have no idea what it might have been. Steve said it sounded like something got dropped. I think they all heard it. I can't wait to get the report back and see if they found any evidence from that night."

A big thank you to Vicky and Phil. It was great to finally meet them in person and I had a really great experience. PIM was very thorough, professional, and easy to work.

Elsing's 2nd Hand Shop is located at 421 East Main Street.

You can reach PIM at their Web site: www.paranormalmilwaukee.com.

***Opposite*: Orb(s) captured during investigation.** *Photo courtesy Elsing's 2nd Hand Shop, Phil and Vicky Elsing.*

City 136: Sun Prairie

Sacred Hearts of Jesus & Mary Catholic Cemetery

I have never seen so many cross-shaped headstones in one place in all my life. Ever.

If you come to this well-manicured cemetery at night, you might see something else. People here after dark have seen orange balls of light, blue balls of light, and other colored balls of light. Even the police have seen these paranormal anomalies.

Sacred Hearts of Jesus & Mary Catholic Cemetery, also known as St. Mary's Cemetery and also as Sacred Hearts Cemetery, is located near the outskirts of town. FYI, famous artist, Georgia O'Keeffe, grew up in Sun Prairie.

Sun Prairie Cemetery

Sun Prairie Cemetery is located on Highway N and Park Street, by day a normal cemetery, by night a playground for the paranormal. Ghosts that look like translucent people have been spotted walking among the gravestones—and through them. A woman and child in white have also been photographed in this Who's Who of Sun Prairie's forefathers. Another oddity: Rumor has it that if you crawl over the tallest grave marker in the Sun Prairie Cemetery at midnight of a full moon, you will be cursed. Hmmm.

A recent investigation by Madison Researchers Into the Paranormal (MRIP) also revealed some strangeness in the back corner of the cemetery. MRIP team members Wayne Hackler and Scotty Rorek (also the hosts of the wildly popular paranormal radio show, Spooks R Us, see the Attractions section) joined me here recently to talk about the cemetery and a recent investigation.

"In July of 2008, Madison Researchers Into the Paranormal was contacted by a third party on behalf of the sexton of the Sun Prairie Cemetery. This cemetery holds the mortal remains of many of the founders and pioneers of Sun Prairie. The cemetery was originally in a different location, and some of the remains were moved in the name of progress to the present location. A few would-be ghost hunters have been in the cemetery after dark (while trespassing) and have had personal experiences and captured some purported evidence," Hackler told me. "I spoke with the sexton at length, and although he's not sure he believes in the paranormal, he was interested in a long-term project to explore the possibility of paranormal activity at the location, with MRIP being

Wayne Hackler and Scotty Rorek.

the only paranormal research group with explicit permission to work the location.

"The six of us were given a tour and a quick history lesson of the cemetery by the sexton. After the sexton left, we split off into teams of three. Team 1 was the stationary monitoring team, consisting of Patrick, Scotty, and myself. Team 2 was the roving team, consisting of Bill, Jessica, and Amanda exploring and documenting the location. Team 1 monitored two locations in the cemetery. The first was a unique monument to one of the city's founders. This was based on the close proximity of the head of this particular family to another family, with whom the individual had a long-running disagreement over education in the fledgling town. Team 2 was assigned the responsibility of doing an investigative survey of the cemetery.

"We were unable to use EMF monitoring devices in the cemetery, due to the close proximity of power lines on the eastern perimeter of the cemetery. We did however monitor air temperature, surface temperature of the monument and humidity. The area was also under surveillance with two video cameras and two digital still cameras using flash filters (to reduce false orbs). Also used was a digital camera with the capability to shoot in the infrared spectrum using nightshot technology. An EVP session was also conducted."

Hackler says, "Later review of the evidence gathered at the monument showed no activity whatsoever. After some time at the monument, Team 1 and Team 2 regrouped at the staging area, with Team 2 giving Team 1 their impressions of their roving survey. The members of Team 2 stated that they believed that the area around the only tomb in the cemetery was active. They had seen moving shadows and felt that they were being watched. During the comparing of notes between the two teams, one member, Jessica, witnessed an apparition from the waist up, approximately twenty-five feet away from us, walk and disappear behind a tall tombstone near the aforementioned tomb. None of the rest of the team members noticed. Because she is so sweet and polite, she didn't want to interrupt the conversation to tell us of what she witnessed. It was really quite humorous. We made sure to tell her that if this happened again, please, feel free to interrupt us."

Team 1 set up using the same equipment as at the monument, focusing on the tomb. Patrick had to leave early, leaving only Scotty and myself on Team 1. Team 2 went back to the roving survey. Scotty and I were sitting near the tomb, near the video cameras, having a light conversation regarding our show. We both heard a guttural growl and the sound of tramping of underbrush (that didn't exist where the sound was heard) by something large. It startled both of us, enough for both of us to say, 'What the hell was that?' in unison. Neither Scotty nor myself could identify the sounds. Review of the videos revealed nothing corresponding to what we heard. But the time in question, on review of the audio portion of the video record, a faint scream could be heard. We were unable to tie the noise to any team member, nor did any of the members hear any screaming at anytime from within or outside the cemetery. Immediate investigation of the noise that Scotty and I heard revealed no animal of sufficient size to cause the noise, nor any persons near the site. The area where we heard the audible noises is at the back of the cemetery atop a steep, cleared hill."

Hackler told me these preliminary findings at the Sun Prairie Cemetery were enough to warrant, in their eyes, a long-term project at the cemetery.

This cemetery has a lengthy history of paranormal activities. Hackler and Rorek pointed out a grave that has continued sinking into itself. This is something I've heard about, but have never seen. It's unnerving and somewhat creepy to say the least.

Sunken grave in the Sun Prairie Cemetery.

Sun Prairie High School

The Sun Prairie High School is said to be haunted by ghosts with no regard for decorum. Papers, without the help of human hands, are said to fly off tables. Noises that cannot be explained are also a part of the ghost or ghosts' repertoire.

The school's 520-seat Cardinal Theatre is supposedly home to a ghost who likes to hang out. Sun Prairie High School is located at 220 Kroncke Drive for now. The high school will be moving to the Angell Park area in the future and the current high school will be used for grades 8-9. Stay tuned to see if the ghosts move to the new high school or stay put to haunt a younger crowd...

City 137: Ulao

Port Ulao

Pronounced *Yoo-lay-oh*, this is one haunted spot that doesn't get much attention from novice ghost hunters, but has been, and is investigated, by many professional paranormal investigators and groups.

Port Ulao is just north of Milwaukee's city limits, on Lake Michigan's sandy shores. In the mid-1800s, farmers were attracted to the windy countryside along with investors.

James T. Gifford, a wealthy man who once served in the legislature of Illinois thought the area was so beautiful that he bought land along the water and also on the bluff above. He is remembered most for building a 1,000-foot pier that extended into the lake.

He suddenly sold his interests in the area to John Randolf Howe, a Great Lakes captain. John's sister, Jane, joined him in Ulao, along with her husband, Luther Guiteau, and their seven-year-old son, Charles, a boy described as high strung. Charles would later be remembered for spending $15 on a revolver in Washington, D.C., and murdering President Garfield. Guiteau was found guilty and hanged. Is one of the restless spirits that haunt this area Charles Guiteau? Some say yes.

The Mormons are another possibility for the area's haunting reputation. A small group of Mormons settled just north of the pier that once extended into the lake, but left just a few years later. What drove them away from Ulao? Some say their restless spirits haunt this beautiful wild stretch of land just east of Highway 43 on County Trunk Q.

City 138: Waterford

Tichigan Lake Inn

Members of the Chicago Mafia and a former customer are said to haunt this former speakeasy located at 28837 Beach Drive. Lights go on and off, glasses fly off shelves and crash to the ground, blenders blend and then shut off on their own... The ghosts seem to find plenty to amuse themselves with here.

A former customer is said to be responsible for the sound of footsteps on the staircase. How, you might wonder, can anyone be sure it's a former customer? A few seconds after you hear the footsteps, an apparition of said customer appears.

City 139: Wauwatosa

Technology Innovation Center

This building originally opened as an isolation and treatment hospital for those afflicted with tuberculosis in 1915. Back then it was called the Muirdale Sanitorium. It was a haven for those afflicted with tuberculosis for a number of years. Here's a little trivia for you: In the year 1900, tuberculosis was responsible for more than 11 percent of all the deaths in the United States. After there was no longer a great demand for tuberculosis treatment, the building housed the mentally ill. Young ghosts have reportedly been seen on the grounds along with the sounds of weeping. When it closed in 1975, some say it became a place where satanic activity took place. It's rumored that some lost their lives engaged in this very activity—which may be another reason the building is said to be haunted.

Apparitions have been seen here, and there are places on the grounds where some get such feelings of intense unease, they literally get sick to their stomachs.

Others say the apparitions are from a time long ago. The site of the Innovation Center is said to be a Native American burial grounds. The site, located at 10437 West Innovation Drive may look innocent by day, but nighttime is a different story. If you're intent on discovering if the rumors of ghosts are true, try the fifth floor. This is where the most ghostly activity takes place.

City 140: West Bend

RESTAT

RESTAT Prescription Benefit Management Company is located in a beautiful building at 724 Elm Street.

This four-story brick building, built in 1897 in the busy downtown part of the city, has been many things before it was RESTAT: the high school, elementary school, and library.

The ghost is said to be a janitor who worked there during life. Unlike many other janitor ghosts I've run across, this one is said to be very anti-female and definitely not what I'd call jovial or helpful.

The RESTAT ghost only seems to make his presence known to the women in the building. They could tell he was nearby when they were enveloped by a cold draft. The entity also makes the hair on your arms stand on end.

Things go missing here; some attribute it to the not-so-nice ghost; some say it's just a case of employee forgetfulness.

UW-Washington County

The library is considered the most haunted spot on campus. At night, books fall from shelves, lights switch on and off at will, and doors slam.

Custodians know better than most that rumors of ghosts here are more than just rumors. The sounds of slamming, banging, and dropping—as if something just fell—were almost nonstop some nights in some rooms. But when an inspection was made, nothing was found out of place and absolutely nothing had fallen on the floor.

Even more disturbing: Other classrooms that had been locked would be found unlocked and trashed. No matter how many precautions were taken, and no matter how many times others checked to make sure the rooms were locked, they would be found unlocked and a mess on the inside.

One time, a custodian had trouble with the lights going on in one room after he shut them off. This happened repeatedly. He went to ask another custodian to ask if there was something wrong. They both went to check it out. While there, they turned the light off. It turned back on by itself. Finally, when they were about to leave and snapped the light switch off, it suddenly turned back on when they were a few feet away. The two men looked at each other. When the light switch began flipping up and down wildly, the two men took off on a dead run. As the two men reached the corner, they could hear the sound of desks sliding across the floor and crashing, as if they were being thrown.

Another area of the school that students feel the presence of something otherworldly is the bookstore. Students sometimes feel someone breathing down their neck—with not so warm breath. When they turn around, they are alone.

The University of Wisconsin-West Bend in Washington County, is located at 400 University Drive.

Washington County Historical Museum

Visitors have heard the sound of footsteps in front of and behind them when no one was there. The sound of doors opening and closing on their own, is also said to be a regular occurrence.

"I was walking toward the door when all of a sudden it slammed shut. I should say it made a slamming *noise* because it never moved an inch," one recent visitor told me. "What's weird is when I took a step back, the door made a click like it was opening, but it didn't move then, either." The museum is located at 320 South 5th Avenue.

City 141: Wisconsin Dells

Dell House

This old tavern is no longer standing. Built in 1873, it burned down long ago. But like many places, that little detail doesn't seem to mean a whole lot to the spirits of those said to linger here.

The Dell House was built near the Narrows, near a fresh water spring and sandy river beach. It was said to be a rough establishment; it's believed more than one patron found their final resting place in the muddy bottom of the river not far from the Dell House.

When river traffic slowed, the Dell House closed. The abandoned building became a campsite for brave tourists and locals until it met its end in 1910, when it was consumed by fire. But even before it burned, stories of supernatural residents had made their way around the state. The typical sounds of tavern-like cursing and laughing could still be heard though the building even though it was as empty as empty could be. And then there were the inexplicable sounds of breaking glass—and footsteps pounding down the stairs.

When the fire did claim the building, it didn't put the spirits to rest. Those that go to the forested spot where the Dell House used to exit swear they hear whispers and see figures and shadows race past them.

Dungeon of Horrors

This former Ford garage is so haunted that as many as 80 percent of employees have reported feeling the ghostly presence of the former owner.

The former owner of the Ford garage was said to have killed himself with a shotgun blast just as his employees were coming in to work one day, long ago.

These days, the current owner has a hard time keeping employees because of the paranormal activity there which seems to peak in August and also on overcast and/or rainy days.

A haunted house that really is haunted. How cool is that?

Dungeon of Horrors is located at 325 Broadway.

Dungeon of Horrors, Wisconsin Dells.

Showboat Saloon

This bar is popular with the locals and tourists—and ghosts. The main ghost believed to haunt the Showboat is Molly, a former resident of the building. She's as much of a help as she is a hindrance, though. She opens and closes doors, and is also known to play with appliances when people are trying to cook.

Keep your eye on the mirror when you're there. Folks from days gone by have been known to make an appearance, and they aren't talking on a cell phone and wearing a tank top. Their 1800s attire suggests they may have been residents or customers of the establishment. Don't try to stop them to chat, though. They're walking along the bar to the exit. Apparently humans aren't the only ones who have things to do and people to see.

Voices have been heard near the stage area, as if someone invisible is talking. The cellar isn't off limits to the ghostly inhabitants, either. The sound of beer kegs being moved can sometimes be heard. Some

Showboat Saloon, Wisconsin Dells.

employees also report cold spots there, as well as strong feelings of anxiety and nausea.

The Showboat is located in beautiful downtown Wisconsin Dells at 24 Broadway.

4

Attractions and
Of Ghostly Interest

Haunted Bayfield Ghost Walk

Bayfield is hailed as "The Best Little Town in the Midwest." Some say it has the best little ghosts in the Midwest, too. Learn more about them on the Haunted Bayfield Ghost Walk, winner of the 2005 GEMmy Award from the Midwest Travel Writers Association. Your costumed guide will meet you with candle lanterns at the Bayfield Carnegie Library. From there you'll hear Native American legends of ice monsters and haunted islands, learn about the founding fathers who are said to still keep watch over Bayfield, and hear tales of coffins, hearses, and shipwrecks.

Virginia Hirsch, a storyteller, historian, and published writer, hosts the ghost walks most nights, starting at twilight. She leads her group down the shadowy streets of Bayfield, telling many entertaining and downright spooky tales of ghosts of the city. Each tour lasts about eighty minutes. "Dying To Get In—A Spirited Walk Through Bayfield's Cemetery" is an attraction that was added in 2008.

The Ghost Walk runs spring through fall, depending on Hirsch's schedule and also during the Halloween season. Reserve a spot by calling 715.779.0299. For information on the Web, visit: http://bayfieldheritagetours.com/.

Burlington Vortex Conference and Fun Days

The year 2008 is the beginning of what paranormal investigator Mary Sutherland, owner of Sci-Fi Café and Gift Shop and Earth Mysteries Museum in Burlington, hopes is a yearly event. The First Annual Conference and Fun Days, held from October 25 through November 2, covers *everything* paranormal. Thanks, Mary!

Lecturers for the 2008 conference included myself, Stanton Friedman a former nuclear physicist, authors Jerry E. Smith, Dr. Claude

Swanson, Dr. Thomas Horn, Peter Moon, Jerry Pippin and Tecumseh Brown Eagle. Turkish UFO expert, Farah Yurdozu, spoke on UFOs and shapeshifters.

The conference also included merchants and outdoor vendors, tarot card and physic readers, art and trade fair, book an DVD signings, haunted bus tours, tour to the haunted woods, scavenger and treasure hunts, dance and Halloween party, moms 'n tots costume contest, Halloween parade, and kids matinee and midnight movie.

Sutherland hopes the event turns out to be an even bigger event than Roswell. I would not be surprised.

To learn more about the conference, Sci-Fi Café, Earth Mysteries Museum, or haunted tours, contact Mary Sutherland by phone: 262.767.1116 or by e-mail: bsutherland@wi.rr.com. The Sci-Fi Café and Gift Shop and Earth Mysteries Museum are located at 532 North Pine Street in historic downtown Burlington.

Burlington Vortex Tours

Walking Day Tours of Historical Burlington Burlington, Wisconsin, is a ghost hunter, orb photographer, ley hunter, historian, and ancient mysteries researcher's dream. Why? Because Burlington, Wisconsin lies on a "rainbow vortex" and is home of the ancient mound builders. Mary Sutherland writes on her Web site, "Just like in the movie *Poltergeist*, they built the town and never moved the bodies. As far as we can determine, the downtown area of Burlington, Wisconsin, was built over twenty-seven ancient burial mounds. Local newspapers have reported unearthing the remains of human bones while digging foundations for several buildings in the historical downtown area. Human bones were also found on the old fair grounds where the Burlington Blanket Co. originated, and is located near Tower Hill on Storle Avenue, the northeast side of the Fox River (now the old Burlington Mill)."

The Walking Day Tour, which lasts four hours, also takes you to Voree, outside the town of Burlington. It was in Voree that the Prophet James Strang discovered the famous Mormon Brass Plates in a hillside beneath the roots of a giant oak tree.

Also on the tour is Burlington's White River, once known as "The River of the Dead." Its name was coined due the Mormon practice of baptism through proxy at this river. The Mormons favored this river above all rivers, being that the river runs "north." All rivers run south except those that are controlled by the gravitation pull of a large vortex.

In the area where the baptisms took place lies a hidden "serpent mound." Its location was only known to a small handful of residents in Burlington, one of which is Burlington Research Center.

Not only are there ongoing reports of ghostly phenomenon and opening of portals or gateways to dimensional worlds being reported by residents of Burlington, an ancient tunnel system runs under the town. "Most of the entrances to these tunnels have been sealed off, but we are hoping someday to find other entrances open for us to explore and document," she says. Mary writes, "One of our favorite spots to stop and grab a bite to eat is the remnant of an old speakeasy that is now called Coach's Sports Bar and Grill. This, along with the Burlington Research Center, are the only two places in town that are open for public viewing of the underground tunnel entrances. While Coach's can show the sealed entrances, the Burlington Research Center provides a partial opening that you can actually step inside and get an idea how they were constructed. Sorry folks...the tunnel is sealed at each end, so we can't go exploring into the lower recesses. Both places are quite haunted and manifestations of ghostly apparitions are frequent and common—so bring your cameras!"

For more information about the Haunted Tours of Burlington, please contact Mary Sutherland by phone: 262.767.1116 or by e-mail: bsutherland@wi.rr.com. The Sci-Fi Café and Earth Mysteries Museum are located at 532 North Pine Street in historic downtown Burlington.

** A personal note: I took this tour and highly recommend it.

Dinner with the Dead

Stacy Kopchinski of Chances Restaurant in Rochester doesn't mind sharing. The years 2008 marks the beginning of an annual event she will host called Dinner with the Dead in honor of the building-full of ghosts that are said to reside at Chances.

Every Wednesday in October, Stacy will serve a four-course meal to a maximum of forty people along with a big side dish of the rich history of the building. Dinner with the Dead will be held on the second floor of the building. Stacy recently got this unused part of the building ready for the event. As a bonus, she will also hold a special Halloween Night event that will feature appetizers and drinks.

Best of all, you can take pictures and EVPs while you're there!

For more information, contact Stacy Kopchinski, Chances Restaurant, 205 West Main Street in Rochester. Phone: 262.534.2772.

Ghost Tours of Door County

Door County Trolley, Inc.'s Ghost Tours of Door County is a popular tourist attraction in Door County.

You are invited to "step aboard the 'Trolley of the Doomed' as we share tales of ghostly sunken ships, haunted lighthouses, and mysterious happenings on the darker side of this spirited peninsula." To learn more about what the tour entails, times, and other information, visit: http://www.doorcountytrolley.com/ghostTour.htm.

Haunted Chippewa History Tour

This tour, sponsored by the Chippewa Valley Paranormal Investigations, will help you learn about Chippewa's Falls past. You'll learn about the lawless loggers that once lived here, all the way to the present day hauntings of Chippewa Falls.

The walking tour, is approximately 1.1 miles in length; the information will stay with you long after you've cooled your tired feet. Call 715.379.9977 to learn more.

Mars Haunted House

A Haunted House That's Really Haunted!

This strange story of the Mars Haunted House can be divided into two "haunting" parts. The first part is about a man who murdered his entire family and then shot himself in their apartment. The second part is about turning the same apartment building into a haunted house, after being unable to successfully renovate it because of the ghostly occupants in the upstairs apartment.

The story begins with an ordinary family who lived in an old apartment building, like many other families in Milwaukee in the 1940s. This building was called the Cathedral Mayer-Krom Building and was home to a retail store on the main floor. A portion of the upper floor consisted of small rooms. People came to these rooms to receive affordable medical and dental care. The remainder of rooms in the upper part of the building were used as apartments.

What makes this story so amazing is the fact the Miltons, who lived in one of the upstairs apartments, were so un-amazing. The Miltons kept to themselves and stayed in their apartment most of the time;

no one saw them on the streets much. There were reports of yelling, but this isn't amazing, either. After all, it was a family of six living in close quarters.

No one can be sure, but those close quarters may have a contributing factor to the tragedy that took place that fateful autumn day.

On October 3, 1943, the Milton family ceased to exist in human form. At around 3 pm, Mr. Milton came home. He was unhappy; he'd been fired. He was also intoxicated.

First he argued with his wife. He was still angry when his children arrived home. It was then that events took an ugly turn.

He grabbed a shotgun—loaded—and began threatening his family. Did they react in terror? Did they think Mr. Milton was just letting off steam?

The only thing we know for sure is the grisly events that followed. Mr. Milton accidentally discharged the shotgun. The bullet found its mark in one of his children. What follows defies belief. Mr. Milton, horrified no doubt, decided to cover his mistake...by shooting and killing all six members of his family. He then turned the gun on himself.

This is where part two of the story begins. The South Side upstairs apartment on Mitchell Street, was now empty, but it was not silent or still.

Strange things were happing upstairs. Objects from the offices in the building found their way into the now vacant apartment. Pictures on the wall never stayed straight; heavy furniture moved into the apartment, too, on its own.

If there was a logical explanation, no one could put a name to it. An apparition specialist was even called to the building to see if there was in the apartment than met the eye. As you might imagine, a "ghostly presence" was discovered. Soon after, the living occupants of the rest of the building moved out.

This might have been the end of the story, except this is where Mars Distributing Incorporated enters the picture. They bought the building in September of 1983 and moved in. Though all the living occupants had found lodgings elsewhere, the Miltons had stayed put.

The new owner found hallways in the middle of nowhere, rooms nailed shut, and windows that opened to blank walls. Realizing they would never get tenants with these oddities, they decided to fix the problems.

Attempts to put things right were met with destruction of work already performed. Workers who knew what they were doing began getting injured. Progress was slow; too slow. Mars abandoned Plan A and went to Plan B—use the space for storage.

Plan C went into effect after taking the history of the mansion into consideration. In 1993, Mars turned the mansion into a haunted house.

Visitors to the site of the multiple homicide report odd sensations, including chills. Visitors I spoke to said the hair on their arms and neck stood on end the entire time they were inside the mansion—and they've been in many haunted houses.

Is the Milton family still roaming the upstairs of the house? Would it surprise you?

I recently learned that MARS Distributing is also said to be haunted by people from Milwaukee Area Radio Station. That must be one houseful of ghosts!

The Mars Haunted House is located at 734 W. Historic Mitchell Street, and is open during the Halloween Season.

New London Public Museum

Established in 1917, the museum's permanent collection includes a wide range of artifacts, documents, and rare books.

In 2006, the New London Public Museum (NLPM) put on the "Walking Tour of Historic Homes" and in 2007, the NLPM presented "Voices from the Past Cemetery Walk." In 2008, the "Walking Tour of Historic Downtown" was introduced. The museum's plan is to do home/downtown tours in even years and cemetery walks in odd years.

To contact for upcoming exhibits and programs, phone the museum: 920.982.8500 or e-mail them at: museum@newlondonwi.org.

The museum is located at 406 South Pearl Street, in New London.

Spooks R Us

Spooks R Us is a production of MRIP™, Madison Researchers into the Paranormal™, and is one of the highest rated shows on Para-X Radio. Listen in on Mondays at 9 Central, 10 Eastern. Theme: Potpourri of paranormal hi-jinks, Hosts: Scotty Rorek and Wayne Hackler.

Contact info: Web: http://www.myspace.com/spooksrusradioshow, http://www.madisonrip.com/. Email: spooksrus@live.com. This is not just another paranormal radio show. I know—I was a guest! What fun!

Scotty and Wayne bring a unique blend of information, rumor, and humor. Wayne is the founder of MRIP™, Madison Researchers Into the Paranormal. Scotty is an investigator with MRIP™ and was a comedian for over fifteen years.

The show contains many different segments and a mix of case studies and guests like: Around the Bubbler: Stories from everyday people like you, well maybe not you but others. Spooktacular Newz: The wackiest newz and commentary this side of death. Para Speak: Lean new paranormal words and use them in the chat room and on your next investigation or party. The Good The Bad The Haunted? A chat with paranormal people and not your usual suspects. Case Studies: An insightful look into famous and not so famous cases. Something Little Different: A blend of stand up and improv comedy keeping the paranormal light.

Spooks R Us is getting lots of attention—and it's all good! A recent review of the show from Para-X: "Fast becoming one of our favorite shows is *Spooks R Us* because the hosts Scotty and Wayne are just plain fun. And you can hear they are having a lot of fun doing their new show as it certainly comes through to the audience."

A Theater of Lost Souls

People travel from miles around to visit A Theater of Lost Souls. Visit the Web: http://www.atheateroflostsouls.com:80/ to learn about the legend behind this wildly popular attraction. I'll give you a hint: The legend begins with a cemetery that happens to be located beneath the Winnebago Fairgrounds...

Of Ghostly Interest

Listed below are Wisconsin-based paranormal groups and other groups of interest in no particular order:

Contact founder, Noah Leigh, Paranormal Investigators of Milwaukee (PIM) at: www. Paranormalmilwaukee.com.

Heartland Paranormal Investigations, www.heartlandparanormal.com.

Contact Wayne Hackler or any other member of Madison Researchers Into The Paranormal (MRIP). Web site: http://www.madisonrip. com/.

Mary Sutherland at the Sci-Fi Café and Gift Shop and Earth Mysteries Museum, 532 N. Pine Street in Burlington, WI, 53105, or visit the Web: burlingtonnews.net/burlingtonvortexconference. Phone: 262.767.1116.

Email: bsutherland@wi.rr.com. While you're at it, check out Paranormal BUFO Radio! Mary is a great host.

Ghost Researchers In Madison (GRIM). Contact Terre Sims at terres123@ sbcglobal.net, or 608.345.6477.

Milwaukee Area Paranormal Investigations, or M.A.P.I. Visit them on the Web at: http://www.milwaukeeparanormal.com. E-mail them for more information at: mapi@milwaukeeparanormal.com.

Southern Wisconsin Paranormal Research Group (S.W.P.R.G.) based out of Janesville, http://www.paranormalresearchgroup.homestead.com.

Wisconsin Paranormal Scientific Investigations, based located in southern Wisconsin, http://www.geocities.com/wipsi2000/index.html.

Kindred Spirits Paranormal is a non-profit paranormal research group, http://kindredspiritsparanormal.net/index.html.

James Andrew Aho is a Milwaukee-based paranormal researcher and author. Visit: EARS: Evidence of Alien contact Revealed in Scripture, http://www.thelightside.org/ears to learn more. James is also the original founder of The W Files, an archive of Wisconsin paranormal activity.

Noah Voss, founder of GetGhostGear.com Enterprises. Visit http://www. GetGhostGear.com, http://www.UFOwisconsin.com, and http://www.w-files.com/ to learn more about paranormal investigative equipment and supplies—all that is paranormal in Wisconsin.

Greater Milwaukee Paranormal Research Group. Web site: http://www. gmprg-wi.com/. You'll find a wealth of fascinating information here.

Chippewa Valley Paranormal Investigators. http://www.chippewavpi. com/index.html.

Coulee Region Paranormal Investigation Society. http://www.crpis.org/.

Paranormal Investigators of Kenosha. http://www.kenoshaparanormal. com/moreinvestigations.html.

Fox Valley Spirit Hunters (FVSH), located in east central Wisconsin in the Fox River Valley. Web site: http://fvsh.sillybirds.com/.

Wisconsin/Illinois Paranormal Society (WIPS) is based in Illinois but serves Wisconsin and Illinois. Web site: http://www.w-i-p-s.com/.

Confidential Paranormal Investigators (CPI). Web site: http://www. cpiteam.net/.

Ghost Team Of Antigo. Web site: http://www.ghost-team-of-antigo. com/.

Madison Ghostseekers Society Homepage. Web site: http://hometown. aol.com/ssofsky/homeindex.html.

River Cities Paranormal Society. Web site: http://www.rcpswi.com/.

Wausau Paranormal Research Society. Web site: http://www.pat-wausau. org/.

Milwaukee Ghost Tours & Investigation. Web site: http://www. milwaukeeghosts.com/about.asp.

East Central Wisconsin Paranormal Investigations. Web site: http://ecwpi.
r8.org/. ghost_matt@hot
com.

Great Lakes Paranormal Society. Web site: http://greatlakesparanormal.
i8.com/.

Paranormal Investigation Crew, P.I.C., which operates out of southeastern
Wisconsin. Web site: www.myspace.com/paranormalinvestigationcrew.
Members include: Jason Weckerle, Michelle Landers, Dave Murphy
(Murf), Dave Keifer, Carissa Winters, and Esmerelda Nino. Call Jason
& Michelle at: 414-520-7250 or Dave (Murf) Murphy at: 262-210-
7906.

Bibliography

Bengs, Blair. "Area ghosts spell spooky Friday the 13th." *Student Voice Online.* 12 Oct. 2006. http://www.uwrfvoice.com/index.php/news/article/219/.

Boyer, Dennis. *Northern Frights: a Supernatural Ecology of the Wisconsin Headwaters.* Oregon, Wisconsin: Badger Books Inc., 2005.

Burlington Vortex Tours – Historical Sites. http://www.burlingtonnews. net/hauntedtours3.html.

"Cristy Mansion." The Longest List of the Longest Stuff at the Longest Domain Name at Long Last.

http://thelongestlistofthelongeststuffatthelongestdomainnameatlonglast. com/haunted194.html.

"DW Choices." Discover Wisconsin.

http://www.discoverwisconsin.com/dw_choices/?list=07f0ff054eaf.

Elsing, Vicky. I Am Haunted. http://www.iamhaunted.com/Vicky-E.

Erickson, Randy. "City's ghost sightings faded into the night." *La Crosse Tribune Galleries.* 31 Oct. 2002. http://www.lacrossetribune.com/ar- ticles/2002/10/31/stories/news/z3randy.txt.

Franklin, *Dixie. Haunts of the Upper Great Lakes.* Holt, Michigan: Thunder Bay Press, 1997.

Godfrey, Linda S. and Hendricks, Richard D. *Weird Wisconsin.* New York: Sterling Publishing Co., Inc., 2005.

Ghost Research of Wisconsin. http://www.wighosts.com/.

Hollatz, Tom. *The Haunted Northwoods.* St. Cloud, Minnesota: North Star Press of St. Cloud, Inc., 2000.

The James Sheely House Restaurant and Saloon. http://www.jamesshee- leyhouse.com/.

JFK Prep. http://www.infiltraterz.com/jfk1.html.

Hauck, Dennis. *Haunted Places: Ghost Abodes, Sacred Sites, UFO landings, and other supernatural locations*. New York: Penguin Books, 1994.

Haunted Bayfield Ghost Walk. http://bayfieldheritagetours.com/ghost. htm.

"Haunted: Dartford Cemetery, Green Lake, Wisconsin; Reported November 17, 2007." Topix.com. http://www.topix.com/forum/city/dane-wi/ T54M7O6UE9H1LKDQV.

Haunted Lighthouses. http://paranormal.about.com/od/hauntedplaces/a/ aa061608.htm.

Haunted Places. http://www.haunted-places.com/HPlocations.htm.

Haunted Places in Wisconsin. Shadowlands Haunted Places.

http://theshadowlands.net/places/wisconsin.htm.

The Legend of Madeleine Island. http://library.thinkquest. org/05aug/00689/Pages/MADELEINE_ISLAND.html.

Levy, Hannah Heidi, and Borton, Brian G. *Famous Wisconsin Ghosts and Ghost Hunters*. Oregon, Wisconsin: Badger Books Inc., 2005.

Little Bohemia Lodge and Restaurant. http://www.littlebohemialodge.com/.

New London Public Museum, and Villiesse, Jim. "The Tales of Captain Drummond."

Novitzke, Candice. "Ghost at Amy's Ritz?" *The Chippewa Herald*. 31 Oct. 2003. Chippewa.com.

http://www.chippewa.com/articles/2003/10/31/news/news1.txt.

"A Theater of Lost Souls". Oshkosh Wisconsin Haunted House.

http://www.atheateroflostsouls.com:80/.

Parlin, Geri. "Ghost Stories: Dead but not gone." *La Crosse Tribune*. 28 Oct. 2007.

http://www.lacrossetribune.com/articles/2007/10/28/news/01ghoststories 1028.txt.

Scott, Beth and Norman, Michael. *Haunted Wisconsin*. Minocqua, Wisconsin: Heartland Press, 1980.

Strub, Sherry. *Ghosts of Madison, Wisconsin*. Atglen, Pennsylvania: Schiffer Publishing Ltd., 2008.

Wagenblast, Bernie. (rshsdepot) Ashland.

http://www.railfan.net/lists/rshsdepot-digest/200201/msg00056.html.

Seibel, Jacqueline. "Stirring up the ghosts." 27 Oct. 2004. JS Online..

http://www.jsonline.com/story/index.aspx?id=270099.

Stark, William F. *Ghost Towns of Wisconsin*. Sheboygan, Wisconsin: Zimmermann Press, 1977.

Vivian Hotel. Langlade County, Wisconsin Historical Places, Photographs & People. http://freepages.genealogy.rootsweb.ancestry. com/~antigowis/places/hotels/vivian.html.

Wanie, Michael J. "History of Woodville (Calvin Blood) Cemetery." Paranormal Assessment Team. 2000.

Wauwatosa Landmarks. Milwaukee County Historical Society.

http://www.milwaukeecountyhistsoc.org/historic_landmarks/landmarks_ Wauwatosa.html.

Wisconsinosity. http://www.wisconsinosity.com/.

WIX. http://hauntedwi.com/.

"Your Ghost Hunting Guide: Wisconsin." GhostTraveller.

http://www.ghosttraveller.com/wisconsin.htm.

Index